Longman
Simplified English Series

TALES OF MYSTERY
AND IMAGINATION

LONGMAN SIMPLIFIED ENGLISH SERIES

Longman Simplified English Series

TALES OF MYSTERY AND IMAGINATION

BY
EDGAR ALLAN POE

SIMPLIFIED AND ABRIDGED BY R. JOHN

ILLUSTRATED BY IVAN LAPPER

LONGMAN

LONGMAN GROUP UK LIMITED
Longman House, Burnt Mill, Harlow,
Essex CM20 2JE, England
and Associated Companies throughout the world

First published in this series *1964
New impressions *1964; *1966 (twice);
*1970; *1971 (twice); *1973;
*1974; *1976; *1977 (twice);
*1979 (twice); *1980; *1982;
*1984; *1985; *1986; *1987

Produced by Longman Group (FE) Ltd
Printed in Hong Kong

ISBN 0-582-52891-7

Longman Simplified English Series

This book has been specially prepared to make enjoyable reading for people to whom English is a second or a foreign language. An English writer never thinks of avoiding unusual words, so that the learner, trying to read the book in its original form, has to turn frequently to the dictionary and so loses much of the pleasure that the book ought to give.

This series is planned for such readers. There are very few words used which are outside the learner's vocabulary[1]. These few extra words are needed for the story and are explained when they first appear. Long sentences and difficult sentence patterns have been simplified. The resulting language is good and useful English, and the simplified book keeps much of the charm and flavour of the original.

At a rather more difficult level there is *The Bridge Series*, which helps the reader to cross the gap between the limited vocabulary and structures of the *Simplified English Series* and full English.

It is the aim of these two series to enable thousands of readers to enjoy without great difficulty some of the best books written in the English language, and in doing so, to equip themselves in the pleasantest possible way, to understand and appreciate any work written in English.

[1] The 2,000 root words of the *General Service List of English Words* of the *Interim Report on Vocabulary Selection*.

INTRODUCTION

EDGAR ALLAN POE was an American writer and poet who was born in 1809 and died in poverty in 1849. He was educated partly in England (as he described in *William Wilson*) and partly in America.

He wrote much poetry and was a noted literary critic, but he is best remembered for his many short stories which he wrote while employed by various literary papers. Amongst these *The Fall of the House of Usher* and *William Wilson* appeared in 1839, *The Gold Bug*, *The Murders in the Rue Morgue*, *A Descent into the Maelstrom* and several shorter stories in 1841, *The Masque of the Red Death* in 1842 and *The Cask of Amontillado* in 1846.

Poe had a deep interest in unnatural things, and there is strangeness of one sort or another in all his stories. He also had an extraordinarily clear mind, and he invented a new kind of story—stories about the skilful solution of crimes and less serious puzzles. Since he wrote it in 1841, *The Murders in the Rue Morgue* has been the model for many thousands of such stories.

Although he was the child of actor-parents, Poe was unfamiliar with the theatre; but it is interesting to see that several of the stories in this collection (e.g. *The Fall of the House of Usher*, *The Cask of Amontillado*) have all the qualities of a good play.

CONTENTS

WILLIAM WILSON

IN THIS STORY I shall call myself William Wilson. I am ashamed to tell you my real name which is known, scorned and hated all over the world. Because of my evil life, I no longer enjoy the love and honour of my fellow-men; and I have no ordinary human hopes or expectations.

I shall not describe the later years of my life, which were full of misery and unpardonable crime. I suffered at one time a sudden increase in wickedness. All goodness seemed to drop from me, in an instant, like a wrap. Men usually grow evil by degrees, but I passed at once from simple dishonesty to blackest crime. I want to describe the chance, the one event, that caused this terrible thing. The shadow of death is over me now, and it has softened my spirit. I need the sympathy and perhaps the pity of my fellow-men. I want them to look for something in my story that might lessen the shame of my guilt. I hope they will agree that no one has ever before been tempted as I have. It is certain that no one has ever yielded as I have. At this moment I am dying from the effects of a wild and fearful experience.

My family has always produced men of strong imagination, often of violent temper. And I have some of the worst faults of the family character. As I grew up these faults developed and caused serious anxiety to my friends and great harm to myself. My parents could do little to change my ways, because they themselves had the same weaknesses. Since boyhood, therefore, I have been able to do very much as I liked.

My earliest memories of school life are connected with a large old house in an English village. I was a pupil at this school for five years after my tenth birthday. It was at that time and in that place that I experienced the first uncertain warnings of my terrible fate. The full and active mind of a child needs no outside interests to amuse it; and my schooldays provided more real excitement than pleasure or crime has ever given me.

The unusual qualities of my character soon gave me a position of leadership among my school-fellows. Indeed I gained an influence over all the other boys of about my own age—with one exception. This exception was a pupil who, although not a relative, was also named William Wilson. This was not really very strange, because my name was a common one. In this story I have called myself William Wilson, and this is not very different from my real name. Well, my namesake[1] was the only boy who competed with me in the studies of the class, and in the sports and quarrels of the playground. He alone refused to accept my opinions and obey my orders; and he interfered with my plans in every possible way.

Wilson's resistance annoyed me very much. Although I treated him carelessly in public, I secretly felt that I feared him. I could not help thinking that my endless struggle to avoid defeat proved that he was better than I. Yet none of our companions admitted this; none even suspected that Wilson and I were rivals. I knew that he wanted to keep our competition private. He had none of the ambition or strength of will that drove me on; he wanted no power for himself. His only purpose seemed to be to annoy *me* and spoil *my* success. There were times, though, when I could not help noticing that he showed a certain *sympathy*, perhaps even *love*, towards me. I did not like this behaviour because I thought it meant that he was sorry for me.

It was just an accident that Wilson and I started school on the same day; and, as I have said, he was not connected with my family in any way. But I was astonished when I heard by chance, after leaving school, that he was born on

[1]namesake: a person having the same name as another.

the 19th of January, 1813—which is exactly the date of my own birth.

Although I was always anxious about Wilson, I did not hate him altogether. It is true that nearly every day we had a quarrel, and that he always allowed me to defeat him. At the same time he managed to make me feel that *he* had deserved the victory. We were never violent enemies, but we could never be real friends. It is not easy for me to describe my feelings towards him: they were a mixture of dislike, some regard, more respect, much fear and a great deal of anxious curiosity.

I soon realized that the best way of attacking Wilson was to make fun of him. But he was not easy to make fun of. In fact I was forced to make use of his one particular weakness, in order to keep my leading position. This weakness was his voice. For some reason—perhaps disease of the throat or the organs of speech—my rival could not raise his voice *above a very low whisper*. I showed no mercy, I am afraid, in joking about this unfortunate condition.

Wilson revenged himself in many ways; and he disturbed me more than I can say. One of his habits was to imitate me in every detail, and he did this perfectly. It was an easy matter for him to copy my dress. He soon mastered my movements and general manner. In spite of the weakness in his speech, he even imitated my voice. He could not copy my louder sounds of course, but the *key*—it was exactly mine. After a time his extraordinary whisper became *the perfect model of my own voice*. The success of all this imitation may easily be imagined when I say that we were the same size, and as alike in general appearance as two brothers.

The only comfort that I could find in this situation was that no one else seemed to notice it. Wilson himself was the only one who laughed at me. Why the whole school did not see his plan, watch it being put into action, and join in the laughter, was a question that I could not answer. Perhaps the fact that the imitation became perfect gradually made it difficult to see.

3

Wilson had another habit that made me very angry. He loved to give me advice. He gave it in a way that seemed to suggest that I badly needed it. I did not like this at all, and I resisted it as strongly as I could. Yet I must admit now that none of his suggestions were mistaken or unwise. His moral sense was far greater than my own. Indeed, I might have been a better and a happier man if I had more often accepted him as my guide.

As it was, I grew more and more to dislike his unpleasant interference. But it was not until the end of my stay at the school that I began really to hate him. It was about this time that I had a strange experience with him. We had had a more than usually violent quarrel, and Wilson spoke and acted very openly. I noticed in his voice, his manner and his appearance, something which first surprised me and then deeply interested me. I fancied that I had known him before—in some distant past, perhaps, or in some earlier life. The feeling (it was more a feeling than a thought), faded almost at once; and I mention it now simply because it was the last time I spoke to him at school.

One night, just before I left the school, I decided to try one more joke upon my rival. While everyone was sleeping, I got up and went, carrying a lamp, to Wilson's small room. I opened the curtains around his bed, and saw that he was sleeping. I looked—and a feeling of icy coldness flowed through my body. My limbs shook, the blood seemed to leave my head, and I felt sick with fear. Struggling for breath, I lowered the lamp to his face. Was *this* the face of William Wilson? I saw, indeed, that it was, but I trembled at what I saw. He did not look like this—certainly not like *this*—when he was awake. The same name! the same appearance! the same day of arrival at the school! I thought of his long, long imitation of my walk, my voice, my manner and my habits. Was it possible that Wilson's face, *as I saw it now*, was the result of his long and careful imitation *of my own?* Weakened and unable to think clearly, I put out the lamp and left the room. Before morning came I had left the school, never to return to it again.

A few months later I went to Eton.[1] This change of scene caused me to forget the other school, and I thought no more about my namesake. I lived a very foolish life and hardly studied at all. I shall not describe those three wasted years, during which the roots of evil sank deep into my spirit. My story moves on to the end of that time. One evening, after a week of hard drinking, I invited a small group of my wildest friends to a secret party in my rooms. We met late at night; for our pleasures were to last until morning. The wine flowed freely, but there were other enjoyments too, which brought almost the light of madness to our eyes. The first light of day could already be seen in the east, when the eager voice of a servant was heard outside the room. He said that some person, who seemed to be in a great hurry, wanted to speak to me in the hall.

As I stepped outside into the shadows, I saw the figure of a youth about my own size. He was dressed in a white morning coat just like my own. He rushed towards me, took me by the arm, and bent his head to mine; and then I heard the voice, the low *whisper*, "William Wilson!", in my ear. He raised a finger and shook it violently, as a solemn warning. This movement of his brought a thousand memories racing to my mind—they struck it with the shock of an electric current. And then in a moment he was gone.

For some weeks after this event I made earnest inquiries. I knew, of course, that my unwelcome visitor was my namesake. But who and what was this Wilson? and where did he come from?—and why did he interfere in my affairs? But I could find out nothing of importance about him. I learned merely that he had left that other school, because of a sudden accident in his family, on the same day that I myself had gone.

[1]Eton: a famous English school.

A little later I went to Oxford.[1] Here the foolish generosity of my parents allowed me to continue a life of wasteful pleasure. And it was at Oxford that I learned the evil art of cheating; this shows how far I had fallen from the state of a gentleman. Indeed, it was only the seriousness of this offence that permitted me to practise it. My friends, all of them, would rather have doubted the clearest proofs than have suspected me of such behaviour; for I was the gay, the generous William Wilson.

After I had successfully cheated at cards for two years, a rich young nobleman named Glendinning came to the University. He had a weak character and seemed the ideal person for my purpose. I often played with him, and managed to let him win one or two fairly large amounts of money from me. In this way I drew him deeper into the trap. At last my plan was ready. I met him at the rooms of a friend who knew nothing about my cheating. There were eight or ten young men present. I carefully directed the conversation and succeeded in making Glendinning suggest a game of cards. We played for a long time, and at last he and I sat alone at the table. The rest of the company stood around us looking on. In a very short time Glendinning, who was drinking heavily, owed me a lot of money. Less than an hour later his debt was four times as great. Although this was a very large amount of money, I did not think that such a loss could account for Glendinning's paleness; for he now looked as white as death. His family, I had heard, was one of the wealthiest in England. I thought that the wine had caused him a feeling of sickness. I was about to suggest that we stopped the game, when I was surprised by some remarks from our friends. There was a cry of despair from Glendinning, and I understood at once that I had ruined him completely.

There was silence in the room, and some of those present

[1]Oxford: a famous university in England.

6

looked at me with scorn or blame in their eyes. My face was burning, and I do not know what I might have done, if a sudden interruption had not come. The door of the room burst open, and a violent wind blew out the lamps. Their light, as it died, showed us that a stranger had entered and was now standing among us. And then we heard his voice.

"Gentlemen," he said, in a low, clear and never-to-be-forgotten *whisper*, which brought a lump to my throat, "I do not apologise for this interruption because it is a duty. You do not know the true character of the person who has tonight won a large amount of money from Lord Glendinning. I advise you to examine the inside of his left sleeve[1] and the large pockets of his coat." Then he left the room as quickly as he had entered.

How can I describe my feelings? How can I explain that the *feeling* of guilt is a thousand times worse than the fact? But I had little time for thought. Many hands roughly seized me, and lights were immediately brought in. A search followed. All the picture cards necessary in the game that we had played were found in my sleeve. Several sets of cards carefully arranged to give me always the advantage were also found in my pockets.

My friends received this discovery with silent scorn. And their silence troubled me more than any burst of anger would have done.

"Mr. Wilson," said our host at last, "we have had enough of your skill at cards. I hope you will leave Oxford. At all events, you will leave my rooms at once."

Early the next morning I began a hurried journey to Paris. I felt the bitter pain of shame rising in waves which left me weak.

But *I fled[2] in vain*. My terrible fate followed me, as if with joy. It proved, indeed, that I had only just begun to feel its power. In Paris Wilson again broke in upon my affairs.

[1]sleeve: the part of a coat, etc., that covers the arm.
[2]fled: past tense of *flee* = run away.

Years went by, and I felt no relief. In Rome—at the moment of my success—he stepped in between me and my ambition! In Vienna, too—and in Moscow! I fled again; he followed; to the ends of the earth *I fled in vain*.

Whenever Wilson disturbed any action of mine, he did so with a single intention: to prevent the realization of some plan of mine which might have resulted in serious harm. I gained no comfort from knowing this. I felt only anger over the loss of my natural rights of action. He had continued, for very many years, his successful imitation of my dress. But I had not once since boyhood seen his face. Whatever he was, the hiding of his face seemed to me the greatest foolishness. Surely he knew that I recognized him? He was bound to know that, to me, he was always the William Wilson of my schooldays—the hated rival and competitor. But let me hasten to the end of my story.

By this time I had become a heavy drinker; and the effect of wine upon my temper caused me to lose all patience with my namesake. I was in Rome in the year 18—, and I decided to suffer no longer. One evening I attended a dance at the home of a nobleman. He was a gentleman of great age, who was married to a young, gay and beautiful wife. I had arranged to meet the lady in the garden; I will not tell you the shameful purpose of my plan. I was hurrying there when I felt a light hand upon my shoulder, and heard that low, ever-remembered *whisper* in my ear.

I turned angrily upon him and seized him by the collar. He was dressed, as I expected, exactly like I was, and we both wore swords.

"Devil!" I shouted, "you shall trouble me no longer! Draw your sword!"

He hesitated for a moment. Then, with a low sound, he prepared to defend himself.

It was soon over. I was wild with every kind of excitement. I felt that I could have fought an army. In a few seconds he was at my mercy, and I drove my sword through and through his chest.

My terrible fate followed me to the ends of the earth

At that moment I thought I heard a footstep behind me. I looked around, but there was no one. I then turned to my dying enemy. But I cannot in ordinary language describe the astonishment and the terrible fear that filled me when I looked at him. He was very pale, and there was blood upon his clothes. But in spite of these things, I could see that every mark and every line of his face, every thread of his dress, was in the smallest detail *my own!*

It was Wilson; but he spoke no longer in a whisper. I fancied that I myself was speaking while he said:

"*You have conquered, and I yield. But, from now on you also are dead—dead to the World, to Heaven, and to hope! You were a part of me. In my death, see by this body which is your own how surely you have murdered yourself.*"

THE GOLD-BUG[1]

MY FRIENDSHIP with Mr. William Legrand began many years ago. He had once been wealthy, but a number of misfortunes had made him poor; and to avoid the shame of his poverty, he had gone to live at Sullivan's Island, near Charleston, South Carolina.

He was living there in a small hut, with an old servant called Jupiter, when I first met him. He was an educated man and had unusual powers of mind which interested me greatly. His chief amusements were shooting and fishing, and he was an earnest collector of shells and insects.

One cold afternoon about the middle of October, 18—,

[1]bug: an insect.

I went to the island to visit my friend. On reaching the hut I knocked, as was my custom. Getting no reply, I looked for the key where I knew it was hidden, unlocked the door, and went in. I was glad to see that a fine fire was burning in the stove. I threw off my overcoat, and settled down by the fire to wait for my hosts.

They arrived as it was getting dark, and gave me a most eager welcome. Jupiter hurried to prepare a duck for supper, while Legrand began to describe a strange insect which he had found that afternoon, and which he believed to be of a wholly new kind.

"If I had only known you were here!" said Legrand, "I would have kept it to show you. But on the way home I met my friend G——, and very foolishly I lent him the insect. It is of a bright gold colour—about the size of a large nut—with two black spots near one end of the back, and another, a little longer, at the other. Jupiter here, thinks the bug is solid gold, and I'm not sure that he is wrong . . . "

Here Jupiter interrupted with, "That I do; I never felt half so heavy a bug in all my life."

"Indeed," said Legrand, "you never saw gold that shone brighter than this little thing; but let me give you some idea of the shape." He sat down at a small table, on which were a pen and ink, but no paper. He looked for some in a drawer, but found none.

"Never mind," he said, "this will do." And he took from his pocket a piece of what looked like dirty notepaper, on which he made a rough drawing with the pen. When he had finished, he brought the paper over to where I was still sitting by the fire, and gave it to me. My study of the drawing was interrupted by the arrival of Legrand's dog, which jumped upon my shoulders and covered me with kisses; for I was one of his favourite visitors. When I looked at the paper a little later, I was puzzled at what my friend had drawn.

"Well!" I said, "this is a strange insect. It looks like a skull[1] to me."

[1]skull: the bones of the head.

"A skull!" repeated Legrand. "Oh—yes—well, it may look like that on paper. The two black spots look like eyes, I suppose, and the longer one at the bottom like a mouth."

"Perhaps so," I said, "but, Legrand, you are a poor artist."

"No," he said, a little annoyed, "I draw quite well; at least my teachers used to think so."

"Well, my dear fellow, you must be joking then," I said. "This is a very good skull, but a very poor insect."

I could see that Legrand now looked quite angry; so I handed him the paper without further remark. His bad temper surprised me—and, as for the drawing, it *did* look exactly like a skull.

He took the paper roughly, and was going to throw it into the fire when something about the drawing suddenly seemed to hold his attention. In an instant his face grew red—in another as pale as death. For some minutes he continued to examine the paper, turning it in all directions, but saying nothing. At last he took from his coat-pocket an envelope, placed the paper carefully in it, and locked both in the drawer of his desk.

This strange behaviour of Legrand puzzled me, and I was disappointed that, for the rest of the evening, he remained lost in thought. When I rose to leave, he did not invite me to stay the night, as he usually did, but he shook my hand with more than ordinary feeling.

It was about a month after this (and in the meantime I had seen nothing of Legrand) that Jupiter visited me at Charleston. He brought bad news. His master was ill and in need of help. The sickness, according to Jupiter, was caused by a bite which Legrand had received from the gold-bug on the day when he had caught the insect. Jupiter himself, so it seemed, had escaped the same fate only through taking hold of the creature in a piece of paper. The old man then produced a letter from Legrand addressed to me. I read the message with some fear.

"My Dear ——, Why have I not seen you for so long a

time? I have something to tell you, yet scarcely know how to tell it, or whether I should tell it at all.

"I have not been quite well for some days, and I find the greatest difficulty in getting away from Jupiter, in order to make some necessary journeys among the hills along the coast.

"If you find it convenient, come over with Jupiter. *Do* come. I wish to see you *tonight*, upon business of importance, of the *highest* importance.—Ever yours, William Legrand."

This note caused me great anxiety. What could my friend be dreaming of? What business "of the highest importance" could *he* possibly have? I feared that the continued weight of misfortune had at last brought him to the borders of madness. Without a moment's hesitation, I prepared to go with the servant.

Jupiter, I noticed, was carrying three new spades, which, he said, Legrand had ordered him to buy in Charleston, though for what purpose the old man had no idea at all. "It's the bug, sir," he said to me. "All this nonsense comes from the bug."

It was about three in the afternoon when we arrived at the hut. Legrand looked terribly pale and ill, and his dark eyes shone with a strange unnatural light. At his first words, my heart sank with the weight of lead.

"Jupiter is quite right about the bug. It is of *real gold*, and it will make my fortune," he said seriously.

"How will it do that?" I asked sadly.

He did not answer, but went to a glass-case near the wall, and brought me the insect. It was very beautiful indeed, and, at that time, unknown to scientists. It was very heavy, and certainly looked like gold, so that Jupiter's belief was quite reasonable; but I simply failed to understand Legrand's agreement with the servant's opinion.

"My dear friend," I cried, "you are unwell, and . . . "

"You are mistaken," he interrupted, "I am as well as I can be under the excitement which I suffer. If you really wish me well, you will relieve this excitement."

"And how can I do this?"

"Very easily. Jupiter and I are going on a journey into the hills, and we shall need the help of some person whom we can trust. Whether we succeed or fail in our purpose, the excitement which I now feel will be equally relieved."

"I am anxious to help you in any way," I replied; "but, about the insect, I believe that you are talking nonsense. I want you to promise me, upon your honour, that when this journey is over, you will return home and follow my advice, as if I were your doctor."

"Yes; I promise," said Legrand; "and now let us go, for we have no time to lose."

With a heavy heart I set out with my friend. We started about four o'clock—Legrand, Jupiter, the dog and myself. Jupiter was carrying the three spades; I was in charge of two lamps; Legrand took only the gold-bug, fastened to the end of a long piece of string, which he swung to and fro as he walked. Tears came to my eyes when I saw this last, clear proof of my friend's weakness of mind.

Our path led across to the mainland, and on to the high ground to the north-west. We walked for about two hours, and the sun was just setting when we arrived at a high shelf of land, surrounded by forest and wild, broken country. The place was overgrown with bushes. Legrand went straight towards a great tree, which stood, with about eight or ten others, upon the level ground. This tree was taller and more beautiful than all others which I had ever seen; the wide spread of whose branches threw shadows over its smaller neighbours. When we reached this tree, Legrand turned to Jupiter, and asked him if he thought he could climb it. The old man seemed astonished by the question, and for some moments made no reply. At last, after a careful examination of the tree, he merely said . . .

"Yes, I can climb it. How far up must I go, master?"

"Get up the main trunk first, and then I will tell you which way to go—and here—stop! take the bug with you."

"The gold-bug, master!" cried Jupiter, in some disgust; "why must I take that?"

"Do as I tell you," said Legrand, handing him the string to which the insect was still tied; "now, up you go."

The servant unwillingly took hold of the string and began to climb. This part of the strange business was not difficult; for the tree was old, and its trunk uneven, with a number of good footholds; so that, within a short time, the climber was sixty or seventy feet from the ground.

"Keep going up the main trunk," shouted Legrand, " . . . on this side—until you reach the seventh branch."

In a few minutes Jupiter's voice was heard, saying that he could count six branches below the one upon which he was sitting.

"Now, Jupiter," cried Legrand, with much excitement, "climb out along that branch as far as you can. Tell me if you see anything strange."

When I heard these words, I decided, with great sorrow, that there could now be no doubt of my friend's madness. I felt seriously anxious about getting him home. While I was wondering what was best to be done, Jupiter's voice was again heard.

"I'm getting along, master; soon be near the . . . o-o-oh! Lord God have mercy! what *is* this here?"

"Well!" cried Legrand, highly delighted, "what is it?"

"Why, it's a skull," said Jupiter, "and it's fixed to the tree with a nail."

"Well now, Jupiter, do exactly as I tell you—do you hear?"

"Yes, master."

"Give me your attention, then—find the left eye of the skull, and let the bug drop through it, as far as the string will reach—but be careful and do not let go your hold of the string."

"The left eye, master? Yes, yes, I have it! It's a very easy thing to put the bug through this hole—can you see it there below?"

Indeed we could now see the insect at the end of the string, shining, like a little ball of gold, in the last rays of the setting sun. Legrand immediately took a spade, and cleared with it a circular space, three or four yards across, just below the insect. He ordered Jupiter to let go the string and come down from the tree.

My friend now pressed a small stick into the ground at the exact place where the insect fell. He took from his pocket a long tape-measure,[1] one end of which he fastened to the trunk of the tree at its nearest point to the stick. He then unrolled the tape, so that it touched the stick and continued outwards for a distance of fifty feet. Jupiter went in front of him, clearing away the bushes with a spade. At the point thus reached a second stick was pressed into the ground; and around this the ground was again cleared in a rough circle about four feet across. Taking a spade himself, and giving one to Jupiter and one to me, Legrand begged us to begin digging at once.

To speak the truth, I had no wish for further exercise. I would have refused if I could have done so without disturbing my poor friend. But he was now wildly excited, and I judged it wiser to take the spade with at least a show of goodwill.

By the light of the lamps we dug very steadily for two hours, and reached a depth of five feet without meeting anything of greater interest than soil and stones. Then we rested, and I began to hope that the nonsense was at an end. But Legrand, although clearly very disappointed, wiped his face thoughtfully and began again. We had dug out the entire circle, and now we deepened the hole by another two feet. Still nothing appeared. At last my friend climbed up to the surface, with a look of the bitterest defeat upon his face. He slowly put on his coat, which he had thrown off at the beginning of his work. Jupiter gathered up the tools, and we turned in deep silence towards home.

[1] tape-measure: a long narrow band of cloth used for measuring.

We dug very steadily for two hours

We had taken, perhaps, a dozen steps in this direction, when, with a loud cry, Legrand seized Jupiter by the collar.

"You stupid fellow!" he roared; "you good-for-nothing . . .! speak, I tell you!—answer me this instant—which—which is your left eye?"

"Oh, my God, master! Isn't this my left eye for certain?" cried the old man, placing his hand upon his *right* eye, and holding it there as if afraid that his master might try to tear it out:

"I thought so!—I knew it! hurrah!" cried Legrand. "Come! we must go back." Then, speaking more calmly, he said, "Jupiter, was it this eye or that,"—here he touched each of the poor man's eyes—"through which you dropped the bug?"

"It was this eye, master—the left eye—just as you told me,"—and here it was again his *right* eye that the servant touched.

"All right; that is enough; we must try it again."

We returned to the tree. My friend moved the stick which marked the place where the insect had fallen, to a place about three inches to the westward of its former position. He took the tape-measure again from the tree to the stick, as before, and continued in a straight line to the distance of fifty feet. We now reached a point several yards away from the hole which we had dug. Around this new position another circle was marked, and we again set to work with the spades.

We had been digging in silence for, perhaps, an hour and a half, when we were interrupted by the violent crying of the dog. All at once he sprang into the hole, and tore up the soil madly with his paws. In a few seconds we saw a mass of human bones, forming the remains of two complete bodies. These were mixed with dust which appeared to be decayed clothing. One or two strokes of a spade brought up the blade of a large knife. As we dug farther, three or four loose pieces of gold and silver coin shone in the light of our lamps.

Legrand urged us to continue, and he had hardly spoken

when a large ring of iron appeared; we soon found that this was fastened to a strong wooden box. We worked in earnest, and the ten minutes that followed were the most exciting in my life. The box was three feet and a half long, three feet broad, and two and a half feet deep. The ring was one of six— three on each side—by means of which six persons might have carried the box. But we could not move it more than an inch. Luckily the lid was held shut by only two sliding bars. Breathless and trembling with anxiety, we pulled these back. In an instant a treasure of the greatest value lay shining before us. As the rays of our lamps fell upon the box, the light from a confused heap of gold and jewels flashed upward and brought a pain to our eyes.

I shall not pretend to describe the feelings with which I looked upon that wealth. We said nothing, and made no movement, I suppose, for two minutes. Then Jupiter, as if in a dream, fell upon his knees. He buried his arms up to the shoulders in gold, and said quietly:

"And all this comes from the gold-bug; all from the little gold-bug!"

It was necessary at last to think of moving the treasure before daylight. After a short discussion, we decided to lighten the box by taking out, and hiding in the bushes, more than half of the heavier pieces. Leaving the dog to guard them, we hurried away with the box. After an extremely tiring journey, we reached the hut in safety at one o'clock in the morning. We rested until two, and had supper; and then we returned to the hills with three strong bags. A little before four o'clock we arrived at the hole where we divided the rest of the treasure, as equally as possible, among us. We reached the hut, for the second time, with our golden loads, just as the faint light of day appeared over the tree-tops in the east.

After a further rest, we examined and sorted the treasure with great care. We soon found that we now possessed wealth even more immense than we had imagined. In coin there was more than four hundred and fifty thousand dollars. There was not one piece of silver; all was gold of ancient date and of great variety—money from all the countries of Europe. The value of the jewels—the diamonds, pearls and so on—and the hundreds of golden ornaments was more difficult to judge. Their total weight was almost four hundred English pounds. I have not included in this figure one hundred and ninety-seven beautiful gold watches, three of which were worth at least five hundred dollars each. We calculated that the entire treasure was worth a million and a half dollars, but we later found that the actual value was far greater.

The following evening Legrand gave me a full account of this extraordinary event. "You remember," he said, "the piece of paper on which I drew for you a picture of the insect."

"The insect that looked like a skull?" I asked.

"Yes; well, the paper was, in fact, a piece of very fine skin. When you gave it back to me, I, too, saw a skull where I had drawn the bug. But a moment later I saw my drawing on the *back* of the skin. Here, then, was a puzzle; for I was sure that both sides of the skin, though dirty, had been unmarked when I made my drawing.

"That night, after you had gone, and when Jupiter was fast asleep, I tried to solve the puzzle. I remembered that the piece of skin had been found half buried in the sand, near the place where we had caught the insect. Jupiter had picked it up, and used it to take hold of the creature, which he was afraid might bite him. I had wrapped the insect in the skin, and carried it so until we met my friend G——. Then, after lending him the bug, I must have put the skin, without thinking, into my pocket.

"As I sat in deep thought, I remembered another curious fact. It was this: at the place where we had found the insect, I had noticed the ancient wreck of a ship's boat—a few pieces of wood only remained—upon the shore. No doubt you will think me fanciful, but here was a sort of *connection*—a wrecked boat, and, near it, a piece of skin—*not paper*—with a skull drawn upon it. You know, of course, that the skull is the usual sign of the sea-robber—that the figure of a skull is commonly used upon the robber's flag."

"But," I interrupted, "you say that the paper—or skin—was unmarked when you made your drawing of the insect. How, then, did the skull appear, and when did it first appear?"

"Ah, that was the whole mystery; although it did not for long remain one. Every detail of the chain of events came back to my mind. On the evening of your visit the weather was cold (oh, blessèd accident!), and you were sitting close to the stove. Just as I placed the skin in your hand, and as you were about to examine my drawing, the dog entered, and sprang upon your shoulders. With one hand you played with him, while your other hand, holding the skin, must have fallen towards the fire. When at last you looked at the skin, you saw a skull drawn there; but my drawing of the insect was upon *the other side*—the side which you did not look at. It seemed reasonable to me, when I thought about the matter that night, to suppose that the *heat* of the fire had brought out the drawing of the skull. It is well known that certain substances exist by means of which it is possible to write upon paper or skin, so that the letters can be seen only when the paper is heated. The writing disappears, sooner or later, when the material cools, but always re-appears when it is heated.

"To test the strength of this idea I immediately built up the fire, and thoroughly heated the piece of skin. In a few minutes there appeared in the corner opposite to the skull the figure of a small goat—*a kid*. Well, you must have heard of the famous *Captain* Kidd, and I at once believed that the drawing of the animal represented his signature. I say signature, because its position in the bottom right-hand corner of the skin, strongly suggested this idea. In the same way, the skull at the top appeared as a kind of official stamp."

"But was there no message," I asked, "between the stamp and the signature?"

"Not at first; but my belief that some great good fortune

lay near was so strong that I continued the experiment without delay. Heaping wood upon the fire, I warmed some water, and carefully washed the skin. It was coated with dirt, and I thought that this might have something to do with the failure. While it was drying, I thought about Captain Kidd and the treasure that he is said to have buried somewhere along this coast. He was a daring and successful robber, and the stories of his hidden wealth would not have existed so long and so continuously without, at least, *some* truth in them. You will notice that the stories are all about searching *for* money, not about finding it; and this suggested to me that the gold remained buried. I thought that some accident—such as the loss of a note showing its position—might have prevented Kidd or his fellow-robbers from finding it again. I now felt a hope, nearly amounting to certainty, that the piece of skin so strangely found contained a lost record of the place of burial."

"What did you do next?"

"I placed the skin in a tin pan, with the figures of the skull and the kid downward, and put the pan upon the burning wood. In a few minutes, I took off the pan, and examined the skin. To my great joy, the whole was just as you see it now."

Here Legrand, having heated the skin again, as he was speaking, handed it to me. In red print, between the skull and the goat, the following signs appeared:

"53‡‡†305))6*;4826)4‡.)4‡);806*;
48†8§60))85;1‡);:‡*8†83)88)5*†;
46);88*96*?;8)*‡);485);5*†2:*‡)
;4956*2)5*—4)8§8*;4069285);)6†8
)4‡‡;1)‡9;48081;8:8‡1;48†85;4)4
85†528806*81)‡9;48;)88;4)‡?34;48
)4‡;161;:188;‡?;"

"It is beyond my power," I said, returning the skin to him, "to understand what this means."

"And yet," said Legrand, "the solution is not very difficult; for Kidd, as you might imagine, was not a very clever man. The figures and signs have a meaning; and a little practice with puzzles of this sort has made it easy for me to understand them. I have solved others a thousand times more difficult than this.

"The first question that one must usually ask is this: in what language is the message written? In this case it is no problem at all; for the drawing of a goat, or kid, in place of Kidd's real signature, makes it clear that the language used is English.

"The next step is to find the figure, or sign, that appears *most frequently* in the message. I saw immediately that the figure 8 is the most common, but perhaps it is best to count them all if you are in doubt. Now, in English, the most common letter is *e*. Let us suppose, then, that the figure 8, of which there are thirty-three in Kidd's message, stands for the letter *e*. Let us see next if the 8 often appears in pairs—for the *e* is very often doubled in English, in such words, for example, as 'meet', 'speed', 'seen', 'been', 'agree', etc. We find that the 8 is doubled five times in this short piece. We may now feel reasonably sure that the figure 8 represents *e*.

"Of all the *words* in the English language, the most common is 'the'. We should now look at the message to see if we can find any group of three figures or signs, the third of which should be 8, which is repeated in the same order several times. We see, in a few moments, that the group ;48 is repeated, in that order, not less than seven times. We may believe, then, that ;48 represents the word 'the'. We now know that ; represents *t* and that the figure 4 stands for *h*.

"Look next at the last but one appearance of the group ;48—towards the end of the message. We may write the known letters, thus:

$$; 4 8 ;) 8 8 ; 4$$
$$t\ h\ e/t\ .\ e\ e/t\ h$$

23

We have here the word 'the', followed by parts of two other words. I say two, because there is no single word, of six letters, in English, that begins with *t* and ends with *eeth*. By trying all the letters of the alphabet,[1] we find that the missing letter is certain to be *r*, giving us the word 'tree'. The sign), then, represents the letter *r*.

"The group ;48 helps us again if we examine its last use in the message. We see this arrangement:

$$; 4 8 ;) 8 8 ; 4) \ddagger ? 3 4 ; 4 8$$
$$t\, h\, e\, /\, t\, r\, e\, e\, /\, t\, h\, r\, .\, .\, .\, h\, /\, t\, h\, e$$

The missing letters are, quite clearly, *oug*, giving us the word 'through', and we now have three more letters, *o*, *u*, and *g*, represented by ‡, ?, and 3.

"I continued in this way to find the other letters, making full use of those already known to me. I wrote down, for example, the group †83)88, which is not far from the beginning of the note:

$$† 8 3) 8 8$$
$$.\, e\, g\, r\, e\, e$$

This can only be the word 'degree', giving me the letter *d*, represented by the sign †.

"It is hardly necessary, I think, for me to go on with the details of the solution. I have said enough to give you an idea of *how* a solution is reached, and to show you that this particular puzzle was not a difficult one. But in making a practical translation of Kidd's message, I had to correct one or two small mistakes, and make use of my knowledge of this district. Here is my translation:

" 'A good glass in Bessop's Castle in the devil's seat—forty-one degrees—north-east and by north—the main branch of the tree—seventh limb east side—shoot from the left eye of the skull—a line from the tree through the shot fifty feet out.' "

[1]alphabet: the letters A, B, C, etc.

24

"I had heard of a family named Bessop, who were great land-owners, at one time, in this part of the country. I made careful inquiries among the older people of the place, and at last met a woman of great age who had been in service with the family very many years ago. She had heard of such a place as *the castle*, and thought that she could guide me to it. She said it was not a castle at all, but a high rock.

"We found it without much difficulty. It was, indeed, an irregular group of cliffs and rocks—one of the rocks being far higher than the others, and quite like the tower of a castle in general outline. I climbed to the top of this tower, and sat there wondering what should be done next.

"All at once my eyes fell upon a narrow shelf of rock, about a yard below where I sat. It was shaped exactly like the back and seat of a chair, and I had no doubt that here was the 'devil's seat' mentioned in the note. I lowered myself to it, and found that it was impossible to sit upon it except in one particular position. Suddenly I understood the full secret of the message.

"The 'good glass' meant not a drinking glass at all, but a seaman's glass—or telescope,[1] to be used from the only possible sitting position in the 'devil's seat'. And the words 'forty-one degrees—north-east and by north' were directions for holding the glass. Greatly excited, I hurried home, found my telescope, and returned to the rock.

"Judging the angle and the direction as best I could by my watch and the position of the sun, I moved the glass slowly up and down. At last my attention was drawn to a circular opening at the top of a great tree in the distance. In the centre of this opening, I saw a white spot, which, in a moment or two, I recognized as a human skull.

"All was now clear to me. The skull was to be found on 'the main branch, seventh limb, east side' of that particular tree. I had to 'shoot', or drop something, from the left eye of

[1]telescope: an instrument used for seeing distant objects.

the skull to the ground; and then to mark a line from the tree, through the place where 'the shot' fell, and outwards to a distance of fifty feet. Beneath that point, I thought it *possible* that a treasure lay hidden.

"The next day, after some little difficulty, I found the tree, and sent for you; and you know the rest of the adventure as well as I do myself."

"I suppose," I said, "that you missed the treasure, in the first attempt at digging, through Jupiter's stupidity in letting the bug fall through the right eye instead of through the left."

"Exactly. That mistake made a difference of five or six yards in the position of the gold."

"Yes, I see; and now there is only one thing that puzzles me. How do you account for the bones found in the hole?"

"There seems only one way of accounting for them—and yet it is terrible to believe in such cruelty. Kidd must have had help in burying the treasure. Then, when the work was finished, perhaps he thought it better that no one should share the secret with him. A couple of shots, while his men were busy in the hole, may have been enough; perhaps it required a dozen—who can tell?"

THE FALL OF THE HOUSE OF USHER

ALL THROUGH a dull, dark and silent day in the autumn of the year, I had travelled alone, on horseback, towards the House of Usher. As I came in sight of the place, my spirits sank; they grew as dark and dull as the sky above me, and as sad as the cold, grey walls of the building before my eyes.

I did not know the reason for this feeling of extreme misery, unless it resulted from the general appearance of decay in the house, and in the grounds which surrounded it. There were the great dark windows, like black eyes in an empty face. The white trunks of lifeless trees stood out upon the banks of a lake, whose still waters reflected the scene above. The reflection seemed even more sorrowful than the reality. In the end I gave up my attempts to solve the mystery of my feelings. I left the lake, and went on to the house.

The owner of the property, Roderick Usher, had been the closest of my childhood friends, but some years had passed since our last meeting. He had recently sent me a very urgent invitation to visit him—had begged me, in fact, to stay with him for several weeks. He wrote that he was suffering from a severe illness, a disease of the mind. My companionship, he thought, would cheer him, and bring calm to his troubled thoughts. He was so sincere about all this, and much more, that I did not hesitate in the matter; and here I was, at The House of Usher.

Although, as boys, we had been the best of friends, I really knew little about Roderick Usher. I remembered that he had always been very quiet, and liked to keep himself apart from other people. His ancient family had been noted, through the centuries, for a peculiar sense of imagination; and this had shown itself in many great works of art and music. I knew, too, the very curious fact that there were no branches to the family of Usher. All its members lay in direct descent; and the name and possessions had merely passed, without any interruption, from father to son. "The House of Usher" meant, to the people of the district, not only the house and land but also the family.

As I drew near the great grey building, a strange fancy grew in my mind. I believed that the air which surrounded the house was different from the rest of God's air. I fancied that it came from the decayed trees, and the grey walls, and the silent lake—that the air itself was grey. It hung about the place like a cloud. I had some difficulty in throwing off this foolish thought.

The house, now that I could see it clearly, looked extremely old. The building was still complete—I mean that no part of the stone-work had fallen; but each separate stone was itself a powdery ruin of what it once had been. There were no other signs of weakness, except a long, narrow crack which ran from the roof of the house in front, right down to the level of the ground.

A servant took my horse, and I entered the archway of the hall. I was then led, in silence, through many dark and winding passages to the master's room. Much that I noticed on the way had a strange effect upon me, although I had been accustomed all my life to objects such as these—the ornamental ceilings,[1] the heavy curtains, the armour and weapons, and the rows of pictures. On one of the staircases, I met the doctor of the family, who seemed both puzzled and frightened by my presence.

The room of my host, which I reached at last, was very large, high and dark. A great deal of ancient furniture covered the floor. Many books and musical instruments lay scattered about, but somehow failed to give any life to the scene. I felt that I breathed an air of sorrow.

Usher greeted me warmly. We sat down, and for some moments I looked at him with a feeling of great pity. Surely, no man had ever before changed so terribly, and in so short a time! He had always been pale—but never so pale as this; his large, bright eyes were now of an unnatural size and of an astonishing brightness; his lips had become a mere line upon his face; the fine, soft hair now floated, uncut, like that of an old man, about his face and neck.

The changed manner of my friend was equally striking. He was, all the time, in a state of high excitement or of great anxiety. As he passed quickly from one to the other of these

[1]ceiling: the inside roof of a room.

conditions, his voice changed: the wild, high note would drop suddenly to a steady, careful sound, like the speech of a man who has drunk too much.

It was in this way that he spoke of my visit, of his earnest desire to see me, and of the comfort that he expected me to bring him. He began a long description of his disease. It was, he said, a family evil, for which there seemed to be no remedy —a simple illness, he immediately added, which would doubtless soon pass. He suffered much from a sharpness of the senses. He could eat only tasteless food, and wear only a certain kind of clothing. He could not bear the smell of flowers. The faintest light brought a pain to his eyes; and he had forbidden all sounds in the house, except those from certain musical instruments.

"I am afraid of the future," he said; "not the events of the future, but their effect upon me. I tremble at the thought of any, even the smallest, happening, which may increase my anxiety. In this terrible state I feel that the time will soon come when I must give up body and soul together, in some personal struggle with FEAR."

It was a great shock to me to learn that he had not left the house for many years. "The house," he said, " . . . the actual walls and towers of the building—have gained an influence over me, a strange power that binds me to them, as if they were living creatures." I did not know what answer to make to my friend.

He admitted, although with hesitation, that much of the unhappiness which he suffered had a simple, almost natural, origin. It was the long and severe illness of a tenderly loved sister—his close companion for many years—his last and only relative on earth. "She is very soon to die," he said, with a bitterness which I can never forget, "and her death will leave me the last of the ancient family of Usher." While he spoke, Lady Madeline (for that was her name) passed slowly through the room at the far end. She did not notice that someone was with her brother. I looked at her with astonishment and deep fear, but I cannot account for these feelings. As soon as she had gone, I turned to my friend. He had covered his face with his hands to hide a flood of tears.

The disease of Lady Madeline had defeated the skill of her doctors, and she no longer cared whether she lived or died. A gradual but continuous loss of flesh caused a weakness of the body, which was made worse by the frequent *stopping* of the heart's action. With great sorrow, my friend told me that there was nothing to distinguish these attacks from real death. "She has now to remain in bed," he said, "and I do not think that you will see her alive again."

For several days following my arrival at the house, neither of us mentioned her name. During this time I made great efforts to comfort and cheer my friend. We painted and read together; or I listened, as if in a dream, to the music which he played. We grew closer and closer in friendship, and shared our most secret thoughts. But all was useless. Darkness poured from his mind upon all the objects around us, in one endless flood of misery.

I shall always remember the many solemn hours I thus spent alone with the master of the House of Usher. Yet I cannot properly explain our studies and activities in words. He was a man of high ideals which had become confused during his long illness. He could now express these ideals only in colour and sound—in the wildest kind of painting, and in difficult music of his own composition. The results were not clear even to himself. It may be imagined how hard it was for me to understand them!

I thought that in one of his pictures the idea was a little clearer, although I myself could not understand it. I have remembered that picture because it caused me to tremble as I looked at it. It showed an immensely long passage, with low walls, smooth and white. The background suggested that the passage was very far below the surface of the earth, but there was no way out of it that I could see. No lamps were shown, nor any other means of light; yet the whole scene was bathed in a stream of bright rays.

During one of our discussions, Usher told me that he believed all plants had the power of feeling. He also thought that even lifeless objects would have this power under certain conditions. As I have already mentioned, this belief was connected with the grey stones of his home. He thought that the way they were arranged in the walls, and had been arranged for hundreds of years, gave them a life of their own. The waters of the lake, too, and the dead trees, shared this life, he said. "The proof," he added, " . . . the proof of *feeling* in the walls and in the water—can be seen in the gradual yet certain development of an air of their own about them." I remembered my thoughts as I had come near the house, and I caught my breath. "This air has had a silent and terrible influence on my family," he said, "and it has made *me* what I am." I could think of nothing to say to my friend.

One evening Usher informed me, in a few words, that Lady Madeline was dead. It was his intention, he said, to keep her body for two weeks, before burial, in one of the many rooms below the house. His reason for this decision was not unnatural, for he had taken into account the peculiar kind of disease from which she suffered. In plain words, he wished to be sure that she was really dead before he placed her body in the family grave.

At the request of Usher, I helped him in making these arrangements. We two alone carried the body, in its coffin,[1] to a small, dark and damp room, lying below that part of the building where I myself slept. It had been used, in the troubled times of long ago, as a store-room for gunpowder, or some other dangerous substance. Part of its floor, and the whole of a long archway through which we reached it, were lined with copper. The heavy iron door was protected in the same way.

Having placed the coffin upon a low table, we partly turned

---

[1]coffin: a box to hold a dead body.

aside its lid and looked upon the face inside. I immediately saw that brother and sister were exactly alike. Usher, guessing my thoughts, said that they had been twins,[1] and that extra-ordinary sympathies had always existed between them. There was a slight colour about her face and neck, and a faint smile— so terrible in death—upon her lip. We did not look at her for long, but put back and fastened the lid, closed the iron door, and made our way back to the upper parts of the house.

It was after three or four days of bitter sorrow, that I noticed a change in the manner of my friend. His ordinary activities—his music, books and painting—were neglected or forgotten. He wandered from room to room, doing nothing, and interested in nothing. He grew more pale than ever, and the brightness left his eye. Sometimes I thought that there was a secret which he wished to tell me, and that he lacked the courage to tell it. At other times he sat for hours, listening with great attention to some imaginary sound, as if expecting something unusual to happen. Is it any wonder that his condition filled *me* with fear—that I felt the wild influences of his own terrible beliefs spreading to *me*?

On the seventh or eighth night, following the death of Lady Madeline, I experienced the full power of these feelings. For hours I lay awake, struggling against a sense of fear. I blamed my surroundings—the dusty furniture, the torn curtains which moved to and fro in the wind of a rising storm, the ancient bed upon which I lay. But my efforts were useless. At last, thoroughly afraid, I got up and looked earnestly into the darkness of the room. I heard—or thought that I heard— certain low sounds that came, from time to time, through the pauses of the storm. I dressed quickly, for I was trembling; but whether with cold or fear I do not know. To calm myself I walked quickly to and fro across the room.

I had done this two or three times, when there was a gentle knock at my door, and Usher entered, carrying a

[1]twins: two children born at one birth.

lamp. There was a look of mad excitement in his eyes.

"And you have not seen it?" he cried suddenly, "you have not—but, wait! you shall." Saying this, and carefully shading his lamp, he hurried to one of the windows, and threw it open to the storm.

The force of the wind that entered nearly lifted us from our feet. But it was not the wind that held our attention, nor the thick clouds that flew in all directions about the house. We had no view of the moon or stars. But the building, and all the objects around us—even the clouds above—were shining in a strange, unnatural light. This light *poured* from the walls and from the waters of the lake.

"You must not—you shall not look at this!" I said, as I led him from the window to a seat. "This light, which troubles you, is merely an electrical disturbance of the air. Let us close the window; for the wind is cold and dangerous to your health. Here is one of your favourite books. I will read, and you shall listen; and so we shall pass this terrible night together."

I began to read, and Usher listened, or appeared to listen, with great attention. It was a well-known story by Sir Launcelot Canning. After I had been reading for eight or ten minutes, I reached the part where the chief character forces his way into the home of his enemy. Here, it will be remembered, the words of the story are:

"And Ethelred lifted his sword, and struck the door with heavy blows. He cracked, and broke, and tore it apart. The noise of the dry and hollow-sounding wood seemed to fill the forest."

At the end of this sentence I paused. I thought that I could hear, though faintly, just such a noise, like breaking wood. It seemed to come from some distant part of the house. It must have been, I believed, some damage caused by the storm; and I decided at once that there was nothing in it to interest or disturb me. I continued the story:

"Then the good Ethelred, entering through the door,

stood upon a floor of silver, in front of a fierce beast. Behind the beast a great shield of brass hung upon the wall. On the shield these words were written:

Who enters here, a conqueror has been;
Who kills the beast, the shield shall win;

and Ethelred lifted his sword again, and struck the head of the beast. With wild and terrible cries, which shook the walls, the beast fell dead, and the heavy shield crashed to the floor at the feet of Ethelred."

Here again I felt astonished and afraid, and was forced to stop my reading. There was now no doubt at all that I *did* actually hear a faint, yet clear, cry of pain. It was closely followed by the distant sounds of metal being struck. I was not sure that Usher had himself heard these sounds, and I rushed, trembling, to the chair in which he sat. His eyes were fixed upon the door; his lips were moving; and, as I bent over him, I heard the words.

"Do I hear it?—yes, I hear it, and *have* heard it. Long—long—long—many minutes, many hours, many days, have I heard it—yet I dared not—oh, pity me, miserable creature that I am!—I *dared* not speak! *We have put her living in the coffin!* Did I not tell you that my senses were sharp? I *now* tell you that I heard her first movements many days ago—yet *I dared not speak*. And now—tonight—Ethelred—ha! ha!—the breaking of the door, and the death-cry of the beast, and the crashing of the shield!—say, instead, the forcing of her coffin, and her cries and struggles in the copper archway of her prison! Oh where shall I hide? Will she not soon be here? Is she not hurrying to scold me for my haste? Have I not heard her footstep on the stair? Can I not feel the heavy beating of her heart? MADMAN!" here he sprang to his feet, and cried aloud the words—"MADMAN! I TELL YOU THAT SHE NOW STANDS OUTSIDE THE DOOR!"

As if in the force of his voice there was some special power, the great door opened. It was the work of the rushing wind—but then outside the door there DID stand the tall, white-

The tall, white-clothed figure of Lady Madeline

clothed figure of Lady Madeline of Usher. For a moment she remained trembling at the doorway; then, with a low cry, she fell heavily inward upon her brother. The shock brought death to Usher in an instant, and a moment later his sister died beside him.

I fled from that room and from that house in fear; and I did not look back until I had passed the lake. A great noise filled the air. As I watched, the crack—the crack that I have spoken of, that ran from the roof of the building to the ground—widened like the jaws of some immense creature. The great walls broke apart. There was a loud shouting sound—the voice of a thousand waters—and then the deep, dark lake closed over the ruins of the "House of Usher".

THE RED DEATH

THE "RED DEATH" had killed thousands of people. No disease had ever been so terrible. Blood was its god and its distinguishing mark. There were sharp pains, and sudden faintness, and much bleeding through the skin; death came in half an hour. Red stains upon the body, and especially upon the face, separated the sufferer from all help and sympathy; and as soon as these signs appeared, all hope was lost.

But Prince Prospero was happy and brave and wise. When half his people had died, he called together a thousand of his lords and ladies, all in good health, and with these went to live in his most distant castle. The immense building, and its extensive lands, were surrounded by a strong and high wall. This wall had gates of iron. The nobles, having entered, heated and melted the locks of the gates, and made sure that no key would ever open them again. The castle, which no one could now enter or leave, was well provided with food, and safe from the danger of disease. The world outside could take care of itself. Meanwhile, it was foolish to worry, or to think. The prince had planned a life of pleasure. There were actors and musicians, there was Beauty, there was wine. Outside the walls was the "Red Death".

The court had been, perhaps, five or six months at the castle, and the disease outside had reached its height, when Prince Prospero invited his thousand friends to a grand dance. It was to be the most splendid event of the year. Masks[1] were to be worn.

Seven of the best rooms at the castle were specially arranged and furnished for the dance. These rooms were irregularly placed, at a corner of the building, with sharp turns between them; so that it was hardly possible to see into more than one at a time. Each of the rooms was painted, furnished and ornamented in a different colour; and the windows were of coloured glass to match the rooms. The room at the eastern end was coloured in blue —and its windows were bright blue. The second room was furnished in purple, and here the glass was purple. The third was all in green, the fourth in yellow, the fifth in orange, and the sixth in white. The seventh room was entirely black, but its windows were different. They were the only ones that did not match the colour of the room. The glass here was red—a deep blood colour.

Now there were no lamps or lights inside any of these rooms. But *outside* each of the coloured windows, fires had been lit, and threw their rays inwards, producing a number of strange and wonderful appearances. But in the black room the effect of the fire-light that shone through the red glass was terrible in the extreme. Few of the company were bold enough to enter this room.

In this seventh room a great clock of black wood stood

[1]mask: a small piece of silk used to cover the upper part of the face.

against the western wall. Whenever the time came for this clock to strike the hour, it produced a sound which was clear and loud and deep and very musical, but of such a peculiar note that the musicians stopped their playing to listen to it. Thus the dancing was interrupted, and there were a few moments of confusion amongst the whole gay company. Then, when the last stroke had ended, a light laughter broke out. The musicians looked at each other and smiled at their own foolishness, saying that they would certainly not allow the striking of the clock to interfere with their music at the next hour. But, an hour later, there would be another pause, and the same confusion as before.

In spite of these things, it was a gay party. There was beauty and originality in the dresses of the ladies, and much that was bright and imaginative in the clothing of the noble lords. There were some who appeared terrible, and a few who might have caused a feeling of disgust. The masked dancers moved to and fro in the seven rooms, like figures in a dream. They moved in time to the music and changed colour as they passed from one room into the next. It was noticeable that, as the evening passed, fewer and fewer went near the seventh room—the black room, lit by the blood-red rays.

At last the great clock in this room began to strike the hour of midnight. And then the music stopped, as I have said; and the dancers stood still; and there was a feeling of discomfort amongst all. Before the last of the twelve strokes had sounded, several of the more thoughtful dancers had noticed in the crowd a masked figure, whom no one had seen before. His appearance caused first a whisper of surprise and dislike, that grew quickly into cries of fear, and of disgust.

The figure was tall and thin, and dressed from head to foot in the clothing of the grave. The mask which covered the face was made to look so like that of a dead body, that even the closest examination might not easily have proved it false. And yet the company present did not really object to this. Their dislike and disgust arose from the fact that the stranger had imitated the *Red Death*. His coverings were marked with blood—and over the whole face were the *red stains* of death.

When the eyes of Prince Prospero fell upon this terrible figure (which, with a slow and solemn movement, walked to and fro among the dancers) his face reddened with anger.

"Who dares," he demanded loudly of the nobles who stood near him, "who dares insult us in this way? Seize him and tear off the mask—so that we may know whom we have to hang at sunrise!"

The prince was standing in the eastern or blue room, as he said these words, with a group of his particular friends by his side. At first there was a slight movement of this group towards the strange figure, who, at the moment, was also near; but no one was willing to put out a hand to seize him. He walked, without interference, past the prince, through the blue room to the purple—through the purple to the green—through the green to the yellow—through this again to the orange—and even from there into the white room, before any firm movement was made to stop him. Then Prince Prospero, maddened with anger and the shame of his own momentary cowardice, rushed hurriedly through the six rooms, drawing his sword as he went. The figure had reached the western wall of the seventh—the black—room, when he turned suddenly towards the prince. There was a sharp cry—and the sword fell to the floor; the next instant Prince Prospero fell dead beside it. Then, with the wild courage of despair, a crowd of the noble lords threw themselves upon the stranger, who stood silent and still in the shadow of the great black clock. They tore at the mask of death and the blood-stained clothing—and fell back, trembling with fear. There was no human form or body to be seen. The mask and the clothes were empty.

And now they knew that their visitor was the Red Death. He had come like a thief in the night. And one by one the

Prince Prospero fell dead beside it

dancers dropped and died in those halls of pleasure. The black clock struck once, and stopped. And the flames of the fires died out. And Darkness and Decay and the Red Death held power over all.

THE CASK[1] OF AMONTILLADO[2]

I HAD SUFFERED, as best I could, the thousand wrongs that Fortunato had done to me, but when he began to be insulting I swore to revenge myself. I did not, of course, threaten to kill him. I waited for my chance patiently. I wanted to avoid the risk of failure; and if revenge is to succeed, two conditions are necessary. The wrong-doer must know that he is being punished, and by whom; and it must be impossible for him to hit back.

I continued to treat Fortunato kindly and to smile in his face. He did not realize that my smile was at the thought of how I would sacrifice him.

Fortunato had one weakness, although on the whole he was a man to be respected and even feared. He was very proud of his knowledge of wine. In other respects, he merely pretended to be wise, but on the subject of wine he was sincere. We shared this interest. I knew a great deal about the Italian wines myself, and bought large amounts whenever I could.

My chance came one evening during a holiday. We met in the street. He had been drinking heavily, and he greeted me very warmly. He was dressed for the Feast, in a striped

[1]cask: a barrel.
[2]Amontillado: an expensive Spanish wine.

suit and a tall, pointed cap with bells. I was so pleased to see him that I thought I should never finish shaking his hand.

I said, "My dear Fortunato, how lucky I am to meet you today. I have received a cask of what is said to be Amontillado, but I have my doubts."

"Amontillado?" he said. "A cask? Impossible! And in the middle of the Feast!"

"I have my doubts," I replied; "and I was foolish enough to pay the full Amontillado price without asking you for advice. I could not find you, and I was afraid of losing a bargain."

"Amontillado!"

"I have my doubts, but I would like to be sure."

"Amontillado!"

"As you are busy, I am on my way to Luchresi. He will be able to tell me . . . "

"Luchresi cannot tell Amontillado from any other kind of wine."

"And yet some fools say that his taste is a match for your own."

"Come, let us go to your wine-store."

"My friend, no. Perhaps you have nothing to do, but I see that you have a very bad cold. My wine-store is far below the ground, and it is very damp."

"Let us go, anyhow. The cold is nothing. Amontillado! You have been deceived. And as for Luchresi, he cannot distinguish a Spanish from an Italian wine."

Saying this, Fortunato took my arm. I put on a mask of black silk, and, lifting the high collar of my coat, I allowed him to hurry me to my house.

My servants were not at home. I had told them that I should not return until the morning, and had given them strict orders not to leave the house. I knew that these orders were enough to make them all disappear, as soon as my back was turned.

I took two lamps from their stands, and, giving one to Fortunato, led him through a dozen rooms to the archway that opened on to a long, winding staircase. At the foot of this stood the wine-store of my family, the Montresors.

The step of my friend was unsteady, and the bells upon his cap rang as he walked.

"The cask?" he said; and he burst out coughing.

"It is farther on," I said. "How long have you had that cough?"

My poor friend was unable to answer me for several minutes.

"It is nothing," he said, at last.

"Come," I said firmly, "we will go back. Your health is precious. You are rich, respected, admired, loved; you are happy, as I was once. You may be ill, and I cannot be responsible. We will go back. There is always Luchresi . . . "

"Enough," he said, "the cough is nothing. It will not kill me. I shall not die of a cough."

"True—true," I replied. "Indeed, I did not wish to frighten you—but you should take care. Here, a drink of this will defend us from the damp."

I knocked off the neck of a bottle of fine old wine which I took from a long row that lay on the damp floor.

"Drink," I said, handing him the wine.

He raised it to his lips with a smile. "I drink," he said, "to the dead that lie around us."

"And I to your long life."

He again took my arm, and we went on.

"This store," he said, "is extensive."

"The Montresors," I replied, "were a great and numerous family."

The wine made his eyes shine, and the bells rang. We passed between long walls of piled up bones—the ancient remains of my family. We passed row after row of bottles and barrels.

"The damp increases," I said. "We are below the bed of the river."

I broke and handed him another bottle of wine. He emptied it almost at once. His eyes flashed with a fierce light. He laughed and threw the bottle upwards.

"Let us see the Amontillado," he said.

"Yes, the Amontillado," I replied.

We went on through several low arches, down a dozen steep steps, continued, and reached at last a deep cave. Here the air was so bad that our lamps gave far less light than before. At the end of this cave, another smaller one appeared. Its walls had been piled to the roof with human remains, as the custom was many years ago. Three sides of this farther cave were still ornamented in this way. The bones had been thrown down from the fourth side, and lay in a heap upon the floor. The bare wall showed yet another opening, in depth about four feet, in width three, in height six or seven, which had been cut into the solid rock. The faint light from our lamps did not allow us to see into this small space.

"Go in," I said; "here is the Amontillado. As for Luchresi . . ."

"He is a fool," interrupted my friend, as he stepped unsteadily forward, while I followed close behind. In a moment he had reached the wall, and found his progress stopped by the rock. He stood still, puzzled, and wondering what to do. A moment more and I had chained him to the rock. In its surface were two iron rings, in a horizontal line, about two feet apart. A short chain hung from one of these, and a lock from the other. Throwing the chain around his waist, I fastened the lock in a few seconds. He was too much astonished to resist. Taking out the key, I stepped back to the entrance.

"Feel the wall," I said. "Indeed, it is very damp. Once more let me *beg* you to return. No? Then I must leave you. But I must first do all I can to keep out the cold air from your little room."

"The Amontillado!" cried my friend.

"True," I replied; "the Amontillado."

As I said these words I walked across to the pile of bones

I had chained him to the rock

in the middle of the floor. Throwing them aside, I uncovered a quantity of building stone and mortar,[1] and some tools. With these I began quickly to build a wall across the entrance to the little space.

I had laid the first row of stones, and had started the second, when a low cry came from inside; and this was followed by by a wild shaking of the chain. The noise lasted for several minutes. I stopped work, and sat down upon the stones in order to listen to it with more satisfaction. When at last the chain became silent, I continued my work, completing the second, third, fourth, fifth, sixth and seventh rows of stones, without interruption. The wall was now up to the level of my chest. I paused again, and held my lamp over the stone-work, letting its weak rays fall upon the figure inside.

Violent cries burst suddenly from the throat of the chained form. They seemed to force me back from the wall. For a brief moment I hesitated, I trembled; but I remained firm. I went on with my work. I replied to the shouts of my friend. I repeated his sounds—but louder. I did this, and at last he grew quiet.

It was now midnight, and I had reached the eleventh row —the last row—of stones. In a few minutes only a single stone remained to be fitted and plastered in. I struggled with its weight. I placed it partly in position. But now there came from inside a low laugh that made the hairs stand upon my head. It was followed by a sad voice, which I could hardly recognize as that of Fortunato. The voice said:

"Ha! ha! ha!—a very good joke, indeed—an excellent joke. We shall have a good laugh about it—he! he! he!—over our wine!"

"The Amontillado!" I said.

"Ha! ha! ha!—yes, the Amontillado. But is it not getting late? They will be waiting for us—Lady Fortunato and the rest. Let us go."

---

[1]mortar: material used for joining stones in building.

"Yes," I said, "let us go."

"For the love of God, Montresor!"

"Yes," I said, "for the love of God!"

There was no reply to this. I called and called again; and at last I heard a ringing of the bells upon his cap. My heart grew sick; it was the dampness, of course. I forced the last stone into position, and plastered it up. Against the new wall, I piled up the bones. For half a century no one has disturbed them.

THE WHIRLPOOL[1]

WE HAD REACHED THE TOP of the highest rock, and now stood about fifteen or sixteen hundred feet above the angry seas that beat against the sharp, black cliffs of Lofoden. The old man was so out of breath that for some minutes he could not speak.

"Not long ago," he said at last, "I could have guided you here as well as the youngest of my sons; but not now. Now I feel broken in body and soul. Three years ago I suffered a terrible experience—such as no other human being has lived to describe. I passed through six hours of the worst fear that you can imagine; and in that time I grew old. In less than a day my hair changed from black to white, my limbs became weak, and all courage left me. I have brought you here so that you might have the best possible view of the scene of my suffering—and to tell you the whole story with the place just under your eye."

[1]whirlpool: water turning round very quickly.

"We are now," he continued, "very near the coast of Norway, and this rock that we are on is called Helseggen, the Cloudy. Sit down and look out on to the sea."

A wide stretch of dark, almost black, ocean lay below us. To the right and left, as far as the eye could reach, stood lines of sharp-pointed rocks. A narrow band of white water marked the point where they entered the sea. About five miles out to sea there was a small, bare island. About two miles nearer the land, there was another of smaller size, surrounded by a ring of dark rocks. The appearance of the ocean, in the space between the more distant island and the shore, had something very unusual about it—a short, quick, angry crossing of the water in every direction, both with and against the wind.

"The farther island," went on the old man, "is called Vurrgh. The nearer one is Moskoe. Do you hear anything? Do you see any change in the water?"

As the old man spoke, I noticed a loud and gradually increasing sound, like the noise of a hundred windmills. At the same moment I saw that the movement of the sea below us was rapidly changing into a current that ran eastward. Even while I looked, the speed of this current increased almost beyond belief. Within five minutes the whole sea as far as Vurrgh was stirred into terrible violence; but it was between Moskoe and the coast that the main disturbance lay. Here the wild waters, lifting, racing, roaring, turned and twisted in a thousand circles, and all rushed on to the eastward with fearful speed.

But in a few minutes the scene changed again. The surface grew smoother, and the whirlpools, spreading out to a great distance, combined to give birth to another. Suddenly—very suddenly—this could be clearly seen in an immense circle more than a mile across. The edge of the whirlpool was represented by a broad belt of white water. The whirl itself, as far as it was possible to see, was a smooth, shining, ink-black wall of water, sloping at an angle of about forty-five degrees to the horizon. Round and round it flew, sending out to the winds a frightening voice, half cry, half roar, like nothing ever heard upon earth.

The rock on which we were sitting trembled to its base. I threw myself flat upon my face, and held tight to the stone.

"This," I said at last to the old man "...this *can* be nothing else than the great whirlpool of the Maelström."

"So it is sometimes called," he said. "We call it the Moskoe-ström, from the island of Moskoe."

The ordinary account of this whirlpool had certainly not prepared me for what I saw. The description given by Jonas Ramus, which is perhaps the best, does not in any way equal the reality; but perhaps he did not see it from the top of Helseggen. Some of the details that Ramus gives are interesting, although they are hardly strong enough to express a clear idea of the wonder.

"When the tide is coming in," he says, "the stream runs rapidly up the coast between Lofoden and Moskoe. When it is going out, the roar is not equalled even by the loudest and most terrible waterfalls. The noise is heard several miles away. The whirlpool is of such an extent and depth, that if a ship comes too near, it is pulled into the circle and carried down to the bottom, and there beaten to pieces against the rocks. Then, when the tide turns, the broken parts are thrown up again. The length of time between the tides, when the sea is more or less calm, is seldom more than a quarter of an hour, after which the violence gradually returns."

This attempt of Jonas Ramus to explain the whirlpool as an action of the tides seemed reasonable enough to me, when I first read it many years ago. But now, with the thunder of the depths in my ears, it seemed quite unsatisfactory. As I looked upon the scene, my imagination accepted the belief of Kircher and others. They thought that there is a hole or crack, *running right through the earth*, and opening out, at the other end, in some distant part of the ocean. I mentioned this idea, as a joke—for it is foolish in the extreme—to my guide.

49

I was surprised to hear him say that most people believed it, although he did not himself.

"You have had a good look at the whirl now," he said, "and if you creep round this rock, away from the noise, I will tell you a story. It will prove to you that I ought to know something about the Moskoe-ström."

We moved round the rock, and he continued.

"My two brothers and I once owned a sailing-boat of about seventy tons, with which we were in the habit of fishing beyond Moskoe, nearly to Vurrgh. In all violent currents at sea there is good fishing, if one has only the courage to attempt it. But among the whole of the Lofoden seamen, we three were the only ones who made a regular business of going out to the islands, as I tell you. The usual fishing-grounds are a long way to the southward. We took the risk of the whirlpool for the sake of the fine fish that were to be caught in large numbers about the rocks of Moskoe.

"It was our practice to sail across to the islands, far above the pool, in the fifteen minutes of calm between the tides. There we would fish until the next calm, about six hours later, when we made our way home. We never set out without a steady wind for going and coming back. In six years of fishing we failed only twice to calculate the weather correctly. On both of these occasions we found safety near the islands.

"We always made the crossing of the Moskoe-ström itself without accident: although at times my heart has beat wildly when we happened to be a minute or so behind or before the calm. My eldest brother had a son eighteen years old, and I had three strong boys of my own. These would have been a great help at such times, in using the oars; but, although we ran the risk ourselves, we hated the thought of taking the young ones into danger; for it *was* a terrible danger, and that is the truth.

"It was almost three years ago, on the tenth of July, 18—, that we experienced along this coast the most terrible storm that ever came out of the heavens. Yet all the morning, and indeed until late in the afternoon, there was a gentle and steady wind from the south-west, and not a cloud was to be seen.

"The three of us—my two brothers and myself— had crossed to the islands about two o'clock in the afternoon. We soon loaded the boat with fine fish, which, we all agreed, were more plentiful that day than we had ever known them. It was just seven, by my watch, when we started for home, so as to reach the Ström at calm water. We knew the calm would be at eight o'clock.

"For some time we went along at a great rate, never dreaming of danger, until suddenly, without any warning, the wind dropped, and we could make no progress. At the same time, a strange copper-coloured cloud, moving at great speed, came up behind us. We had little time to wonder what to do. In less than three minutes the storm was upon us, and it became so dark that we could not see each other in the boat.

"It would be foolish of me to attempt to describe that storm. The oldest seaman in Norway had never known anything like it. At its first breath, my younger brother was blown straight into the sea and lost. I should have followed him if I had not thrown myself flat, and held on to an iron ring in the middle of the boat.

"For some moments we were entirely under water, and all this time I held my breath. When I could bear it no longer, I raised myself on to my knees, still holding the ring, and thus got my head clear. Then our little boat gave herself a shake, just as a dog does in coming out of the water, and partly got rid of the seas. The next instant I felt a hand upon my arm. It was my elder brother, and my heart jumped for joy, for I had thought that he was surely drowned; but at once my joy was turned into fear—for he put his mouth close to my ear, and shouted out the word '*Moskoe-ström!*'

"No one will ever know what my feelings were at that moment. I shook from head to foot, as if I had the most violent fever. I knew what he meant by that one word well enough—I knew what he wished to make me understand. With the wind that now drove us on, we were going straight towards the whirlpool of the Ström, and nothing could save us, unless we reached it at the time of calm.

"We had lost our sails, and the boat was now out of control, racing through mountainous seas, such as I had never seen in my life. A change had come over the sky, although in every direction it was still as dark as night. For a moment I was puzzled, but then, directly above us, a circle of clear blue sky appeared. In this circle I saw the full moon shining, lighting up everything around us—but, oh God, what a scene it was to light up.

"I now tried to speak to my brother, but he could not hear a single word; for the noise had, for some reason, greatly increased. He shook his head, and held up one of his fingers, as if to say '*listen!*' I did not quite understand what he meant.

"Suddenly a terrible thought came to me. I pulled out my watch. It was not going. I looked at its face in the moonlight, and then burst into tears as I threw it far out into the ocean. *It had stopped at seven o'clock! We were behind the time of the calm, and the whirlpool of the Ström was now in full force!*

"A little later a great wave carried us with it as it rose—up—up—as if into the sky; and then down we swept with a rush that made me feel sick. But while we were up, I had taken a quick look around—and that one look was enough. I saw our exact position in an instant. The Moskoe-ström whirlpool was about a quarter of a mile in front of us. I closed my eyes with the worst feeling of fear that I have ever experienced.

"It could not have been more than two minutes afterwards, when we entered the broad white belt that surrounded the whirl. The boat made a sharp half turn inwards, and raced off in its new direction like an arrow. The wind and the waves dropped. The roaring of the water changed to a high whistling sound—like that of a thousand steam-ships, all letting off their steam together. I expected, of course, that in another moment we should dive to the bottom of the whirl. We could not see down into the pool because of the astonishing speed with which we were carried along. The ocean that we had left now rose at our side, like an immense turning wall between us and the horizon.

"Now that we were in the jaws of Death, I made up my mind to hope no more; and when I had reached this decision, I began to think how wonderful it was to die in such a way—surrounded, as we were, by this glorious proof of God's power. It may seem to you like madness, and perhaps it was the madness of despair, but I felt a wish to explore the depths of the whirlpool. My greatest sorrow was that I should never be able to tell my companions on shore about the mysteries that I should see.

"How often we travelled around the edge of the pool it is impossible to say. We circled for perhaps an hour, getting gradually nearer and nearer the terrible inside edge of the white belt. Below us the water sloped away at a steep angle. All this time I had never let go of the iron ring. My brother was now at the back of the boat, holding on to a small empty water-barrel, which was tightly fastened down by a rope. This was the only thing that had not been blown away when the wind first struck us. On our last journey around the pool, before the drop into the depths, he rushed across to me. In great fear—the fear of a madman—he forced my hands from the ring, and took it himself. I never felt deeper sorrow than when this happened, although I knew that it could make no difference in the end; so I let him have the ring, and went back myself to the barrel. I had hardly made myself safe in my new position, when the boat made a wild turn inwards, and rushed down into the whirling depths. I said a short prayer to God, and thought that all was over.

"As I felt the sudden fearful drop, I tightened my hold upon the barrel, and closed my eyes. For some seconds I dared not open them—for I expected immediate destruction. I wondered why I was not already in my death-struggles with the water. About a minute passed. I was still alive. The sense of falling was gone. I took courage, and opened my eyes.

"Never shall I forget the scene around me. The boat seemed to be hanging half-way down the inside surface of a circular, V-shaped hole, more than half a mile across, and of immense depth. Its walls of black water, as smooth as polished wood, were spinning round with terrible speed. The rays of the full moon streamed in a flood of golden glory along these walls, and far away down to the bed of the ocean.

"At first I was too confused to notice more than just the general view, but in a moment or two I saw that the water was at an angle of about fifty degrees to the horizontal. The boat lay evenly on the slope—that is to say, in her ordinary sailing position, relative to the water; and because of the great speed at which we were moving, I had no difficulty at all in keeping my foothold.

"Our first sliding fall into the whirlpool had carried us, as I have said, about half-way down; but after that our progress to the bottom became very much slower. Round and round we swept, each circle taking us a yard or so lower.

"Having time to look around, I was surprised to see that our boat was not the only object in motion. Both above and below us could be seen pieces of boats, tree trunks, and many smaller things, such as boxes, barrels and sticks. I must have been, I think, only partly conscious at this time; for I felt amused, while waiting for death, by trying to guess which object would be the next to dive to destruction. 'That log of wood,' I said at one time, 'will certainly disappear next.' And then I was disappointed to see that the wreck of a merchant-ship passed it and reached the bottom first. I had made several mistaken guesses of this kind before an idea came into my head—an idea that made my limbs tremble again, and my heart beat heavily once more.

"It was not a new fear that I felt, but the birth of a more exciting hope. My faulty guesses had one clear meaning: a large object travelled faster down the whirlpool than a small one. It seemed possible to me, as I watched, that many of these smaller things, whose downward speed was slow, would never reach the bottom. The tide would turn, and bring the whirlpool to an end, while they were still circling its walls. They would then, I supposed, be thrown up to the surface of the ocean, and carried away by the current.

"While I considered these matters, I observed that a short, though very thick, tree trunk, which had been at one time on a level with us, was now high up above. Each time we passed it, the gap grew wider.

"I hesitated no longer. I decided to tie myself to the water-barrel which I was holding, to cut it loose from the boat, and to throw myself with it into the water. As best I could, by means of signs, I explained this plan to my brother, and pointed to the floating logs that came near us. I think he understood— but, whether he did or not, he shook his head in despair, and refused to move from his place by the ring. Action was now urgent; I could not afford to delay. Greatly against my will, I left him to his fate. Fastening myself to the barrel by means of the rope which tied it to the boat, I rolled into the sea without another moment's hesitation.

"The result was exactly what I hoped it might be. As I am now telling you this story, you see that I did escape— in the way that I have described. In the next hour our boat went down to a great distance below me. I saw it make three or four wild turns in the space of half a minute; and then, carrying my loved brother, it dived at once and for ever, into the angry water at the bottom of the pool. The barrel to which I was tied had sunk no more than half-way to the rocks below, when a great change could be seen in the sea around me. The slope of the sides of the whirlpool became every moment less and less steep. The circular movement of the water grew, gradually, less and less violent. Slowly the bottom of the well seemed to rise up towards me. The sky was clear, the wind had died down, and the full moon was

55

I rolled into the sea without a moment's hesitation

setting in the west, when I floated up to the surface of the ocean. I was above the place where the whirlpool had been. It was the time of calm, but the sea was still rough from the effects of the storm. The strong current carried me away down the coast, far down to the fishing-grounds. A boat picked me up; the seamen were my old companions from Lofoden, but no one recognized me. My hair, which had been black the day before, was as white as you see it now. For some time I was unable to speak (now that the danger was over) as a result of my terrible experience, but at last I told them my story. They did not believe it. I have now told it to you— and I can hardly expect you to have more faith in it than they had."

THE PIT[1] AND THE PENDULUM[2]

(*Note:* This is a story of the Spanish Inquisition. The Inquisition was a religious court of law, which, at the time of the story, held power only in Spain. The work of the court was to find and punish people whose religious beliefs and practices did not agree with those of the Church. The punishment was often terribly severe.)

After long hours of suffering, the ropes that bound me were loosened, and I was allowed to sit. I felt that my senses were leaving me. I heard the judges say that I was to die, and then the voices faded. I saw the black clothes of the officials, and the black curtains of the hall. The white lips of

---

[1]pit: a deep hole in the ground.
[2]pendulum: a weight swinging from side to side.

the judges moved; they were ordering the details of my death; and I trembled because I heard no sound. A sudden feeling of sickness filled my body, and a cloud seemed to cover my eyes. Then a thought came to my mind, like a rich musical note—the thought of what sweet rest there must be in the grave. For a moment my eyes cleared, and I saw the judges stand up and leave the room; and then all was darkness and silence and stillness.

I had fainted; but I was not completely unconscious. In the deepest sleep, in fever, even in a dead faint, some part of consciousness remains. Long afterwards, I remembered, though not clearly, that I was lifted up from my seat in the court—that tall figures carried me in silence down—down—and still farther down. At last the movement stopped, as if those who carried me could go no further. After this I remembered something flat and cold and damp; and then misery and great fear.

Very suddenly the sense of motion and sound came back to me. It was the motion of my beating heart, and the sound of its beating in my ears. Then consciousness returned, and later, the power of thought. A trembling fear shook my body, and I felt an earnest wish to know my true state. I made a successful effort to move. I remembered my trial, the judges, and then my faint.

So far, I had not opened my eyes. I lay upon my back, but I was not tied. I reached out my hand, and it fell on something damp and hard. I wanted to look around, yet I dared not; for I was afraid that there would be *nothing* to see. After many minutes of despair, I quickly opened my eyes. The blackness of night surrounded me. I struggled for breath. The darkness seemed like a weight upon me. Where and in what state was I? This was the question that troubled me. Many prisoners, I knew, were put to death in public, and such a ceremony had been held on the day of my trial. Was I being kept until the next sacrifice, which might not happen for many months?

A fearful idea now suddenly sent the blood rushing to my heart, and I trembled in every limb. I stood up and stretched my arms wildly above and around me in all directions. I felt nothing; yet I dared not move a step, for fear that I should be stopped by the walls of a *grave*. I began to sweat, and big cold drops stood upon my face. Taking courage at last, I moved slowly forward, with my arms extended. I walked many steps but felt nothing. I breathed more freely; for, if I had been buried alive, the grave would have been smaller than this.

I went on very slowly, until my hands touched a wall; it was smooth, cold and slightly wet. I followed it, but soon realized that, without some fixed starting point, I should be unable to judge the size of the room. My clothes had been exchanged for a prison wrap, from which I now tore off a strip at the bottom. I placed this piece of cloth, at full length, upon the floor, at a right angle to the wall. I now began to circle the room again. The ground was damp and slippery, and I had hardly taken a dozen steps when I fell forward upon my face. I lay there for some minutes, and felt a great desire for sleep.

I must have slept; for when I woke up, and stretched out an arm, I found beside me a loaf and a bottle of water. I ate and drank eagerly. Shortly afterwards, I continued my walk around the room, and after I had gone about fifty steps, I reached the piece of cloth again. My prison, then, was about thirty yards around, if two of my steps equalled a yard.

There was little purpose—certainly no hope—in having this information; but curiosity urged me further, and I decided to walk across the room to get an idea of its shape. I went carefully, for the floor was very slippery. I had covered perhaps six yards, when the torn edge of my wrap twisted round my foot, and I fell again. Almost at once, I noticed that, while my body rested upon the floor of the prison, there seemed to be *nothing* under my head. At the same time a peculiar smell, like rotting leaves, rose to my nose. I put out my arm, and

I put out my arm

trembled to find that I had fallen right at the edge of a circular pit. I found a small piece of loose stone, and let it fall into the hole. I listened as it struck against the sides; at last, after many seconds, it hit water. A faint ray of light flashed suddenly in the roof above me, and there was a sound like the quick opening and closing of a door. And then all was darkness again.

I now knew the fate which had been prepared for me. If I had taken one more step before my fall, the world would have seen me no more. The death that I had thus avoided was just the kind of death which I had heard of, in stories about the Inquisition. I had laughed at those stories; I had thought of them as fanciful and imaginary. But I now knew that they were true. The Inquisition offered a choice of death: one might die by great bodily pain or by the most terrible moral suffering. And death in the pit would come to me slowly, by the destruction of my mind.

I struggled back to the wall. Shaking in every limb, I imagined other wells in various positions in the room, and other hidden forms of punishment. Thoughts such as these kept me awake for many hours, but at last I slept again. When I awoke, I found another bottle of water and some bread beside me. I drank the water at once, for I was very thirsty. It must have contained something to make me sleep; and I could not keep my eyes open. Unconsciousness, like that of death, must have lasted a long time; but when, once again, I awoke, I could see the objects around me. A bright yellow light shone into my prison, but I could not see from where it came.

The room was roughly square, and of about the size that I had calculated. But the walls, which I had thought were made of stone, seemed now to be iron, or some other metal, in very large plates. The entire surface of this metal room was painted with the figures of devils in the most terrible shapes. Although their outlines were clear enough, the colours seemed to have faded, as if from the effects of the damp. The floor was of stone, and in its centre there was the circular pit, from whose jaws I had escaped. It was the only pit.

I saw all this only by much effort—for my personal position had greatly changed during sleep. I now lay upon my back, at full length, on a kind of low bed. I was tightly bound to this by a long strap or band, which left me free to move only my head and the lower part of my left arm. I could just manage to reach the meat which lay beside me on the floor. The water had gone—and I was more thirsty than ever.

Looking upward, I examined the roof of my prison. It was thirty or forty feet above, and was also made of metal. Directly over my bed the figure of Father Time was painted upon one of the plates. When I first looked at this picture, I thought that the figure held in his hand a large pendulum, such as we see on old clocks. But a moment later the pendulum moved, and I realized that it was not a part of the picture. The movement was short and slow—a slight swing from side to side. I watched it curiously for a few minutes, and then turned my attention to other parts of the room.

I heard a little noise, and saw several large rats crossing the floor towards me. They had come out of the pit which lay on my right side. As I watched, they came up in large numbers, hurrying, with hungry-looking eyes, towards my plate of meat. It needed much effort and attention to frighten them away.

It might have been half an hour, perhaps even an hour, before I again looked up to the roof. What I saw there confused and astonished me. The swing of the pendulum had increased to almost a yard. As a natural result of this, its speed was now much greater. But what mainly disturbed me was the fact that it had come nearer to me. In great fear, I saw that the lower end of the pendulum was formed of a blade of shining steel, shaped like the new moon, and about a foot in length from point to point. The ends of the blade turned upward; and the lower edge looked as sharp as a razor. Like a razor also, it seemed heavy and solid above. It was fixed to a thick rod of brass, and the whole whistled as it swung through the air.

I could no longer doubt the death that had been prepared for me by the human devils of the Inquisition. I had avoided the pit by a mere accident, and I knew that surprise was an important part of the cruelty of these prison deaths. As I had failed to fall, I was not simply to be thrown into the well. A different and a milder destruction was made ready for me. Milder! I trembled as I thought about the word.

What use is it to tell of the long, long hours of suffering that followed, during which I counted the swings of the steel? Inch by inch it fell—down and still down it came! The downward movement was extremely slow, and it was only after several hours that I noticed any increase in the length of the brass rod. Days passed—it might have been many days—before the blade swept so closely over me as to fan me with its bitter breath. The smell of the sharp steel came to me in waves. I prayed for it to reach me quickly. I struggled to force myself upwards against the razor-sharp edge, as it swung across my body. And then I grew suddenly calm, and lay smiling at the shining death, as a child smiles at some bright jewel.

For a short time I lost consciousness. When my senses returned, I felt sick and weak; but in spite of my suffering, I wanted food. With painful effort I reached for the few pieces of meat beside me. As I put some of it to my lips, a half-formed thought of joy—of hope—rushed into my mind. I struggled to make it complete, but it escaped me. Long suffering had nearly killed all my ordinary powers of mind.

The swing of the pendulum was across my body—directly across my heart. It would first touch the cloth of my wrap; it would return and cut deeper—again—and again. In spite of its wide swing (which was now thirty feet or more), and its great speed, it would not, for several minutes, cut into my flesh. At this thought, I paused. I dared not think further. I watched the blade as it flew above me.

Down—steadily down it crept. To the right—to the left—far and wide—with the terrible *whistle* of death! Down—certainly down—within three inches of my chest! I struggled violently to free my left arm. I shook and turned my head at every swing. I opened and closed my eyes as the bright blade flashed above me. Oh, what wonderful relief if I could die!

Suddenly I felt over all my spirit the calmness of despair. For the first time in many hours—or perhaps days—I began to think. The band which tied me was in one piece; but I saw at once that no part of this lay across my chest. There was no hope, then, that the steel would cut the strap, and set me free. Yet, if the strap were broken at one point, I could quickly unwind it from the rest of my body, and slide off the bed. But how fearfully close the blade would be! And how difficult the slightest movement would be, beneath that destroying knife!

Suddenly the unformed half of that thought of hope (that I have already mentioned) came into my mind. The whole idea was now present—weak, unreasonable perhaps—but complete. At once I began my attempt to escape death.

The rats, I hoped, would save me. For many hours they had surrounded my bed. They were wild, bold and hungry, and they had, in the short time that I lay unconscious, eaten nearly all the meat upon the plate. "To what food," I thought, "have they been accustomed in the well?"

For a long time I had kept my left arm moving, to frighten them away, and many had bitten my fingers in their efforts to reach the plate. I knew that if I lay still they would rush upon me. I now took the last pieces of the rich oily meat from the plate, and rubbed them thoroughly into the band wherever I could reach it. Then, resting my hand upon the bed, I lay perfectly still.

In a moment one or two of the boldest sprang upon the bed, and smelt at the strap. This seemed the signal for a general rush. Out of the pit they came in fresh numbers; they climbed upon the bed; I was covered by hundreds of rats. The movement of the pendulum did not disturb them at all. Avoiding its strokes, they tore the strap into which I had rubbed the meat. They pressed upon me. I felt their cold lips against mine; I could hardly breathe for their weight. A

64

feeling of disgust, for which there is no name, swelled my body, and brought a coldness to my heart. One minute more, and I felt the struggle would be over. I noticed the loosening of the strap. I knew that in more than one place it must be already broken. With great determination I lay still.

I had made no mistake—nor had I suffered in vain. At last I felt that I was free. The strap hung in pieces from my body. But the pendulum had already cut through my wrap. Twice again it swung, and a sharp pain ran through my frame. But now the moment of escape had arrived. At a wave of my hand, the rats hurried away. With a steady movement—cautious, sideways, slow—I slid from the bed and beyond the reach of the blade. For the moment, at least, I was free.

Free!—and in the hands of the Inquisition! I had hardly moved from my bed of suffering on to the stone floor, when the movement of the terrible machine stopped, and it was pulled up, by some unseen force, through the roof. I now realized that every action of mine was watched. Free!—I had only escaped death in one form to suffer it in another! I looked anxiously around the walls of iron that shut me in. Something unusual—some change, which, at first, I could not understand, had happened. While I wondered about this, I saw the origin of the yellow light which filled the room. It came from a narrow space, about half an inch in width, which extended around the whole room at the base of the walls. The walls were thus completely separated from the floor. I tried, but of course I failed, to look through this gap.

As I got up from the floor, the mystery of the change in the room became suddenly clear. The terrible figures upon the walls—the paintings whose colours, as I have said, seemed to have faded—now stood out so brightly as to appear living creatures! Their wild eyes shone with fire—real fire; for even while I breathed, the smell of heated iron reached my senses. The walls grew hot, and a faint redness covered the metal plates. I struggled for breath, and rushed to the centre of the room. I thought of the coolness of the pit, and I looked down into its depths. It was lit up by the fire of the burning roof. Yet, for a moment, I refused to believe what I saw in that well of death. Oh! for a voice to speak!—oh! the cruelty of it! Any death—but not the pit! With a cry, I turned from its edge, and buried my face in my hands.

The heat rapidly increased. I was soon forced to look up again; and when I did so, it was to see that the iron walls were moving. Two opposite corners of the room were growing slowly further apart—while the distance between the other pair decreased. The prison was now diamond-shaped—and quickly becoming flatter and flatter. I pressed myself against the wall in my suffering. "Death," I said again, "any death, but not the pit!" Fool! I should have guessed that it was the whole object of those moving walls of fire to force me into the pit. Could I resist their heat? Could I bear their pressure?

At last I knew that I could not. The closing walls pressed me to the side of the well. There was no longer an inch of foothold for my burnt and twisting body on the firm floor of the prison. I struggled no more, but the suffering of my soul found relief in one long, loud and terrible shout of despair. I felt that I trembled upon the edge—I closed my eyes . . .

There was the sound of human voices! There was a loud note, like music! The burning walls rushed back! A strong arm caught my own as I fell, fainting, into the pit. It was that of General Lasalle. The French army had entered the city. The Inquisition was in the hands of its enemies.

THE STOLEN LETTER

IN PARIS, just after dark one windy evening in the autumn of
18—, I was enjoying a quiet smoke with my friend C. Auguste
Dupin, at his home, No. 33 Rue[1] Dunôt, Faubourg St.
Germain. We had been together for perhaps an hour, when our
old friend, Monsieur[2] G——, the Head of the Paris police,
called to see Dupin.

We welcomed him warmly; for he was an entertaining
man—though, in many ways, a fitting object for scorn. We had
been sitting in the dark, and Dupin now got up to light a lamp.
He sat down again, without doing so, when G—— said that he
had called to ask the advice of my friend, about some official
business which had caused him a great deal of trouble.

"If it is something which requires thought," said Dupin,
"we shall consider it with more success in the dark."

"That is another of your curious ideas," said the officer, who
had a habit of calling everything "curious" that was beyond
his power of understanding. He thus lived under a cloud of
curiosities".

"Very true," said Dupin, as he gave his visitor a pipe, and
pushed a comfortable chair towards him.

"And what is the difficulty now?" I asked. "No one has
been murdered, I hope?"

"Oh no; nothing of that kind. The business is very simple
indeed, and I have no doubt that we can manage it quite well
ourselves; but I thought that Dupin would like to hear the
details of it, because it is so very curious."

"Simple and curious," said Dupin.

"Well, yes; but not exactly that, either. The fact is, we have

[1]Rue: Street (French).
[2]Monsieur: Mr. (French).

all been puzzled a good deal because the affair *is* so simple, and yet it has defeated us altogether."

"Perhaps it is just the simplicity of the problem that makes it so difficult for the police," said my friend.

"What nonsense you do talk!" replied G——, laughing loudly.

"Perhaps the mystery is a little *too* plain," said Dupin.

"Well, well! who ever heard of such an idea?"

"And what, after all, *is* the trouble?" I asked.

"I will tell you," replied the officer, as he drew steadily on his pipe, and settled himself in his chair. "I will tell you in a few words. But, before I begin, let me warn you that this is an affair of the greatest secrecy. I should almost certainly lose my position, if it became known that I had told it to anyone."

"Go on," I said.

"Or not," said Dupin.

"Well, then; I have received personal information, from a very high place, that a certain letter of great importance, has been taken from the royal rooms. The person who took it is known; this is beyond doubt; he was seen taking it. It is known, also, that it still remains in his possession."

"How is this known?" asked Dupin.

"It is known because certain results would at once arise if the letter passed out of the robber's possession; that is to say, if he employed it in the way that he must be planning, in the end, to employ it. These results have not yet appeared."

"Tell us more details," I said.

"Well, I may say that the paper gives its holder a certain power in a certain circle where such power is of immense value." G—— was very fond of this official way of speaking.

"Still I do not quite understand," said Dupin.

"No? Well; if a third person, who shall be nameless, should learn what is in the letter, then the honour of another person of the very highest rank would be in doubt. Thus the holder of the letter has power over the distinguished person whose honour and peace are in danger."

"But this power," I said, "would be useless without full knowledge upon both sides. I mean that the loser of the letter would have to know who had stolen it, and the thief would have to know that he was known. Who would dare . . . "

"The thief," said G——, "is the Minister D——, who dares all things. He is as clever as he is bold. The letter had been received by the person, to whom it was addressed, while she was alone in her sitting-room. While she was reading it, the other person—the one who, as I have said, shall be nameless—entered the room. The lady wished especially to hide the letter from him, but she had no time to do so. She was forced to place it, open as it was, upon a table; but the address was uppermost, and the letter itself escaped notice. At this moment the Minister D—— entered. His sharp eye immediately saw the paper, recognized the handwriting of the address, and noticed the lady's confusion. He guessed her secret. After some business matters had been completed, D—— took out a letter from his pocket, opened it, pretended to read it, and then placed it close beside the other upon the table. He then continued, for another quarter of an hour, to discuss public affairs. At last, as he was leaving, he took the lady's letter, and left his own—one of no importance—upon the table. The lady saw all this, but, of course, dared not say anything, in the presence of the third person who stood beside her."

"Here, then," said Dupin to me, "you have full knowledge upon both sides, and D—— has the lady in his power. She saw him take the letter, and he knows that she saw him."

"Yes," said the officer; "and the power thus gained has been used, for some months past, for political purposes, to a very dangerous extent. It becomes clearer to the lady every day, that she must get her letter back. But this cannot be done openly, of course. In despair, she has come to me."

"As you are the wisest agent, I suppose," said Dupin, "whom she could desire or even imagine."

"It is possible that she has that opinion," replied G——.

"It is clear," I said, "that the minister will try to keep the letter. If he used it, he would lose his power over the lady. We must believe that he still has the letter."

"Exactly," said the officer. "I feel so sure that he still has it that I have made a thorough search of his home. It was not easy, because I had to search in secret. I have been warned that it would be very dangerous for me if the minister suspected our plans."

"But the Paris police know very well how to search a house in secret," I said. "They have done this thing often before."

"Oh yes; and for this reason I did not despair. The habits of the minister, too, gave me a great advantage. He is frequently absent from home all night. He has few servants, and they sleep at a distance from their master's rooms. I have keys, as you know, with which I can open any door in Paris. Every night for three months I have personally directed the search. I have promised on my honour to get this letter back; and, although it is a secret, I can tell you that the reward is immense. So I did not give up the search until I was sure that I had examined every hiding place in the house."

"Well, then," I suggested, "the letter may not be hidden in the house at all."

"It probably *is* in the house," said Dupin. "D—— might have to produce it at a moment's notice."

"Have you searched the minister himself?" I asked.

"Yes; my men, pretending to be robbers, have twice searched him thoroughly."

"That was hardly necessary," said Dupin. "D—— is not altogether a fool. He would have expected something like that to happen."

"Not altogether a fool," said the officer, "but he's a poet, and so little better than a fool."

"True," said Dupin, drawing thoughtfully upon his pipe.

"Tell us," I said, "the details of your search."

"Well, the fact is that we searched thoroughly. We took the whole building, room by room, and spent the nights of a whole week in each. We examined, first, the furniture. We opened

70

every possible drawer; and I suppose you know that, to a properly trained police officer, such a thing as a secret drawer is impossible. There is a certain amount of space to be accounted for in every desk or cupboard; and then we have firm rules. Next we took the chairs, and we examined the cushions with the fine long needles which you have seen me use. Then we took off the tops of the tables."

"Why?" said Dupin.

"To see if there was anything hidden in the legs. The bottoms and tops of bed-posts are often used as hiding-places in the same way."

"But surely you did not take all the furniture to pieces. A letter may be rolled up tightly, and pressed into a small hole, for example, in the back of a chair."

"We looked at every part of every piece of furniture with a powerful glass. If there had been anything, such as you suggest, we should not have failed to see it instantly. The smallest grain of wood-dust would have been as clear to us as an apple."

"I suppose you looked at the curtains, the beds and bed-clothes, and the floor coverings."

"Of course; and when we had finished these things, we examined the house itself—every square inch of every floor and wall, both inside and outside."

"You must have had a great deal of trouble," I said.

"We had; but the reward is great."

"Did you include the grounds of the house?"

"All the grounds are of stone or brick. They gave us little trouble. We examined the soil between the bricks, and found no sign of disturbance."

"You looked among D—— 's papers, of course, and into the books of the library?"

"Certainly; we opened every packet and every parcel; we not only opened every book, but we turned over every leaf. We also measured the thickness of every book-cover, and examined each very carefully with the glass."

"You explored the floors beneath the coverings?"

"Yes."

"And the paper on the walls?"

"We did."

"Then," I said, "you have made a mistake, and the letter is not in the house, as you believed."

"I do not know what to think," said G——. "Now, Dupin, what do you advise me to do?"

"To search the house thoroughly again."

"But that is surely unnecessary," replied G——. "As sure as I breathe, the letter is not there."

"I have no better advice to give you," said Dupin. "You have, of course, a full description of the letter?"

"Oh yes!"—And here the officer, taking out from his pocket a little book, read aloud a detailed account of the appearance of the letter. When he had finished this, he left us, lower in spirits than I had ever known him before.

About a month afterwards he called on Dupin again, and found us sitting in the darkness, smoking, as before. He took a pipe and a chair, and began some ordinary conversation. After a little time, I said . . .

"Well, G——, what about the stolen letter? Has the minister defeated you?"

"I am afraid that he has; but I searched again, as Dupin suggested; it was wasted work, as I knew it would be."

"How much was the reward, did you say?" asked Dupin.

"Why, a very great deal—a very generous reward—I don't like to say how much, exactly. But one thing I will say—I wouldn't mind giving my personal cheque for fifty thousand francs[1] to anyone who could bring me that letter. The matter is becoming more and more important every day; and the reward has been recently doubled. If it were doubled again, I could do no more than I have done."

"Oh, you might, I think, do a little more."

"How?—in what way?"

[1] franc: a piece of French money.

"Well, you might employ a good lawyer, for example. Do you remember the story of Abernethy, the doctor?"

"No; what is it?"

"Well, once upon a time a certain rich old man tried to get a free medical opinion from Abernethy. He began an ordinary conversation with the doctor, and pretended that the case was an imaginary one. 'We will suppose,' said the rich old man, 'that the fellow is suffering from . . . ' (and here the old man mentioned the name of his disease); 'now, doctor, what would you have ordered him to take?' "

" 'Take!' said Abernethy, 'why, take advice, of course.' "

"But," said the officer, a little uncomfortable, "I am very willing to take advice, and to pay for it. I would really give fifty thousand francs to anyone who would help me in the matter."

"In that case," replied Dupin, opening a drawer, and taking out a cheque-book, "you may as well write a cheque for me for that amount. When you have signed it, I will give you the letter."

I was astonished. But G—— plainly disbelieved what he had heard. For some minutes he could not speak; he looked at Dupin with open mouth and wide eyes. At last he seized a pen, and, after several pauses, wrote and signed a cheque for fifty thousand francs; he handed it across the table to Dupin. My friend examined it carefully, and put it in his pocket. Then, unlocking the drawer of a desk, Dupin took out a letter and gave it to the officer. G—— took it quickly, opened it with a trembling hand, and read the message. Then he rushed to the door, and out of the room, without saying a single word.

When he had gone, my friend gave me an explanation.

"The Paris police," he said, "are very clever in the ordinary way. They are patient and careful; and these qualities usually bring results. They have one weakness, and G—— is, himself, an excellent example of this: they have no imagination. They never try to imagine what is in the mind of their enemy. Whatever the case, and whoever the enemy, the actions of the police are always the same. G—— and his people frequently fail, first, because they do not try to get inside the mind of the wrong-doer; and second, because they do not measure properly the skill of the enemy. They consider only their own ideas of skill; and, when they are searching for anything hidden, they think only of the ways in which they would have hidden it. G—— believes that all men who wanted to hide a letter would hide it in one or other of the places where he searched: if not in a table-leg, then in a cushion, or between the boards of a floor, or perhaps inside the cover of a book. Now in this case, the police failed really because G—— considered that the minister was a fool; and he considered him a fool because he is a poet."

"But is D—— really a poet?" I asked. "There are two brothers, I know; and both are learnèd. The minister, I believe, has written a good deal on scientific subjects. He is a scientist, and not a poet."

"You are wrong; I know him well; he is both. As poet and scientist, he would be able to reason well. As a mere scientist, he could not have reasoned at all, and would have been at the mercy of the police."

"You surprise me," I said, "by these opinions; but we had better discuss them at some other time. I am very interested now in how you found the letter. Go on."

"Well, I know D—— both as scientist and poet, and I considered him also as a bold politician and as a gentleman of the Court. Such a man would know all about the ordinary actions of the police. He would expect them to search his house. I believe that he stayed away from his home at night on purpose—to give opportunity to the police for thorough search; so that they would decide at last that the letter was not in the building. D——, you see, knew where they would search. He knew that his furniture would be taken to pieces, and that they would look into the smallest and darkest corner of his home. It seemed to me that the minister would be forced to find a simple hiding-place for the letter. You will remember, perhaps, how loudly G—— laughed when I suggested at the beginning, that it was possibly the simplicity of the problem that made it so difficult for him."

"Yes," I said, "I remember very well. He seemed to think that you were joking".

"I was not joking," said Dupin. "Some things are too plain for us to see. There is a game that children are fond of, which is played on a map. One player asks the others to find a certain word—the name of a town, river or state—that is shown somewhere on the map. Now most children choose a name that is written in very small letters; for they think that such a word is harder to find. But a good player chooses a word that stretches, in large letters, right across the map—a word that is *so* plain, in fact, that it escapes notice. It is the same with shop-signs in the street. We stop and struggle to read every letter of the small ones, but hardly look at the big ones. Our friend G—— never thought that the letter would be right under his nose; he never thought that the minister could hide the letter in the best way by not hiding it at all.

"Such a trick, it seemed to me, suited entirely the daring character of the minister; and I decided to prove that my idea was right. Wearing a pair of dark glasses, I called one morning at D——'s house. He was at home, pretending to be tired and too lazy to work, although he is really one of the busiest men in Paris.

"To be even with him, I complained of my weak eyes, and regretted the need for the glasses. While we talked, I looked carefully around the room, but at the same time gave proper attention to the conversation.

"I was very interested in a large writing-table, near which the minister sat. A number of papers and letters, several books and a musical instrument lay upon it; but after a long and detailed examination of this, from where I sat, I could see nothing to cause suspicion.

"At last my eyes, travelling around the room, fell upon an ordinary letter-holder, made of wire. This hung by a dirty blue string from a small brass hook, just above the fire-place.

I talked to D—— for several minutes

In this holder were five or six visiting-cards and one letter. The letter was dirty, and torn across the middle—as if someone had started to tear it up as worthless, but had then decided to keep it. A large stamp showed the arms of the D—— family very clearly. The letter was addressed, in small female handwriting, to the minister himself. It had been pushed carelessly and, it seemed, almost scornfully, into the top of the holder.

" 'This,' I said to myself immediately, 'is what I have come for.' The appearance of the letter was quite different from that of the missing one. But these details—the stamp, the address and the handwriting—could easily result from a simple change of envelope. The dirty and torn condition of the letter, and the careless way in which it lay in the holder, were quite unlike the ordinary tidy habits of D——. I believed that these things might be a part of his plan to deceive the police. When I thought of all this, and saw the letter in full view of every visitor, I had no serious doubts. As soon as I could politely end our conversation, I said good-bye to the minister, and went home. I left my gold cigarette-box on the table.

"The next morning I called for the cigarette-box. I apologised for my forgetfulness, and talked to D—— for several minutes. Suddenly a gun-shot was heard outside the house, followed by a loud cry and the shouts of a crowd. D—— rushed to the window, threw it open and looked out. Meanwhile, I stepped to the letter-holder, took out the letter, and put it in my pocket. I then put another in its place, exactly like it in appearance, which I had carefully prepared at home. Then I followed D—— to the window.

"The trouble in the street had been caused by the behaviour of a man, who had fired an old rusty gun among a crowd of women and children. When the gun was examined, it was found to have powder but no shot, and the fellow was allowed to go. Soon afterwards I left D——'s house. A little later I met the man with the gun, and paid him what I had promised him."

"But why," I asked, "did you put another letter into the holder?"

"You know my political opinions," replied Dupin. "In this matter, I am on the lady's side. For eighteen months the minister has had her in his power. She now has him in hers; for it may be several weeks, or even months, before D—— discovers that he no longer possesses the letter. During this time he will continue to act towards the lady, as if the letter were still in his letter-holder. Sooner or later she will be able to trap him, and cause his political destruction. I have no sympathy for the minister—nor for any clever man who is without honour. I confess, though, that I should like to know D——'s thoughts when, at last, he is forced to open the letter which I placed in his holder."

"Why? Did you write any particular message?"

"Well, it did not seem proper to leave no message at all— that would have been insulting. At Vienna, many years ago, D—— acted rather badly towards me, and I told him, quite pleasantly, that I should remember it. He is bound to feel some curiosity as to who has beaten him; so I decided to help him a little. He knows my handwriting well, and I just wrote in the middle of the paper the words:

A trick so bold,
Requires a bolder one to defeat it."

METZENGERSTEIN

STRANGE AND TERRIBLE events can happen at any time. Why, then, should I give a date to this story? It is enough to say that, at that time, the country-people of Hungary held strong beliefs regarding the human soul. They believed that a soul lived once only in a human body; and that, after death, it passed into the living body of an animal.

The noble families of Berlifitzing and Metzengerstein had been enemies for centuries. The origin of the quarrel seems to be found in the words of an old saying: "A great name shall have a fearful fall when Metzengerstein shall conquer and be conquered by Berlifitzing". The words themselves had little or no meaning—but results, equally strange, have sometimes come from sayings more foolish than this.

The rival families were close neighbours, and they had, for a long time, taken opposite sides in the affairs of a busy government. The high towers of the Castle Berlifitzing, home of the younger and less wealthy family, looked closely upon the windows of the Hall of Metzengerstein. Indeed, one might say that the quarrel was kept alive, and the two houses kept apart, mainly by their nearness to each other.

William Berlifitzing, although of very noble descent, was, at the time of this story, a sick and stupid old man. Two feelings kept him alive: a deep hatred for the Metzengerstein name, and a great love of horses and of hunting. Neither sickness, great age, nor weakness of mind, prevented him from taking part, every day, in the dangers of the hunt.

Frederick Metzengerstein was not yet twenty-one years of age. His father, the Minister G——, died young. His mother, Lady Mary, followed him quickly. Frederick was then eighteen years old. In a city, eighteen years are nothing; but in the country—in so grand a country as I speak of—time has a deeper meaning.

The Metzengerstein possessions were the richest in Hungary. The boundary of the largest park extended for more than fifty miles, and there were numerous castles, of which the Hall of Metzengerstein was the greatest and most splendid.

When Frederick arrived at the Hall to take control of his property, he soon showed his trembling servants, and the quiet country-people of the place, that he was as wicked as he was wild. For three days and nights the wine flowed freely. The shameful behaviour and terrible cruelty of the new master, which had no effect at all on his conscience, reached its lowest point in the evening of the fourth day. The stables[1] of the Castle Berlifitzing were found to be on fire.

While the flames roared, Frederick sat alone in deep thought in one of the upper rooms of the Hall. Great pictures of his ancient family looked down upon him. Here, a group of richly-dressed priests, sitting with some famous Metzengerstein, shook a warning finger at a crowned king, or laughed in the face of some threatening Berlifitzing. There, the tall, dark figures of the Princes Metzengerstein, upon their war-horses, stood in victory over the bodies of their enemies.

As Frederick listened to the noise from the burning stables, his eyes turned by chance to the picture of a great red horse. The animal seemed to fill the picture; for its rider, who appeared only in the background, had fallen by the sword of a Metzengerstein. The dying horseman, Frederick knew, was a member of the rival family; his conqueror stood over him.

An evil expression came to the young man's face, as he looked upon the scene. At last he tried to look away, but his eyes would not obey his will. A feeling of great anxiety came to him, and the longer he looked, the more it seemed to press upon him. The disturbance outside grew suddenly more violent. Frederick forced himself to look at the fierce light of fire which beat upon the windows.

But only for a moment; for at once his eyes returned to the picture on the wall. To his astonishment, the head of the great horse had changed its position. The neck of the animal had before bowed, as if in pity, over the body of its rider; it was now stretched at full length towards the Metzengerstein prince. The large red eyes shone with an almost human expression, and the whole appearance of the beast suggested anger.

Shaking with fear, the young nobleman ran to the door. As he threw it open, a flash of red light streamed into the room;

[1]stable: a building used for keeping horses in.

and Frederick turned to look. He saw his own shadow upon the picture—and it exactly covered the figure of that ancient Metzengerstein prince, the victorious killer of the Berlifitzing horseman.

Frederick rushed into the open air. At the main door he met three servants. With much difficulty, and at great risk, they were struggling to control the wild movements of a great red horse.

"Whose horse? Where did you get him?" cried the young man; for he saw at once that it was exactly like the horse in the picture.

"He is your own property, sir," replied one of the men; "at least, no one else claims him. We caught him flying, blowing and smoking with anger, from the burning stables of the Castle Berlifitzing. Thinking that he belonged to the old man's stable, we led him back there. But they say that he is not one of theirs; which is strange, for he has marks of a narrow escape from the flames. The letters W.V.B. are burnt upon his head, and of course I thought that they meant William Von Berlifitzing—but no one at the castle has any knowledge of the horse."

"Very strange indeed," said the young nobleman. "He is, though, a fine horse—an extraordinary horse. Let him be mine, then. Perhaps a rider like Frederick of Metzengerstein may tame even the devil from the stables of Berlifitzing."

At that moment another servant stepped quickly out of the doorway of the Hall. He whispered in his master's ear an account of the sudden disappearance of a large part of one of the pictures in an upper room. Frederick felt the return of all the strange anxieties that had troubled him earlier, and again an expression of the deepest evil settled upon his face. He gave orders that the room should be immediately locked up, and the key handed to him.

"Have you heard of the unhappy death of the old hunter, Berlifitzing?" said one of the men, as the servant went back into the Hall, and the great horse was led away to Frederick's stable.

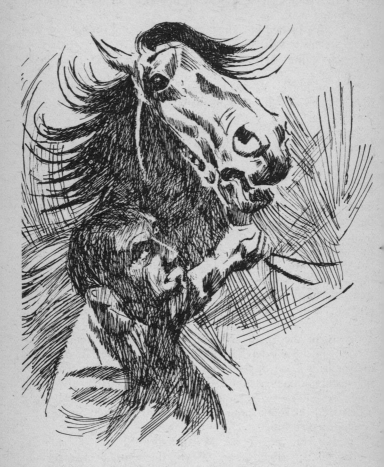

"Whose horse?" cried the young man

"No!" said the young lord, turning quickly towards the speaker, "dead, you say?"

"It is true, sir; and, to a noble of your name, the news will not be unwelcome, I think."

A quick smile appeared on Frederick's face. "How did he die?"

"In a foolish attempt to rescue one of his favourite horses. He died miserably in the flames."

"I-n-d-e-e-d-!" said the young man, as if the truth of some exciting idea slowly entered his mind.

"Indeed," repeated the man.

"Terrible!" said the youth, calmly, and turned quietly into the Hall.

From that time a noticeable change was seen in the behaviour of the young Frederick Von Metzengerstein. He never went outside the boundary of his own land. He kept none of his old friends, and made no new ones—unless that wild, unnatural red horse, which he was always riding, could be called a friend. He refused to attend the social gatherings of the neighbourhood, and took no interest in local affairs. After a time, the invitations that were sent to him became less friendly and less frequent. At last they stopped altogether.

The kindest people thought that young Frederick was unhappy because of sorrow over the early death of his parents; they forgot his terrible behaviour of the first few days. Others felt that he was too proud to mix with his less wealthy neighbours. The family doctor did not hesitate to speak of an unhealthy sadness, from which other members of the family had suffered. There were a few who thought the young man was mad.

Indeed, Frederick's strange love for the great red horse was a very unreasonable state of mind. It grew stronger as the animal gave fresh proofs of its wild nature. In the heat of noon—at the darkest hour of night—in sickness or in health—in calm or in storm—the young Metzengerstein seemed fastened to the saddle of that immense horse.

The speed of the animal, said the people of the villages, was twice that of any other horse. It was an extraordinary thing that no one—except the young lord—had ever touched the body of the beast. Even the three men who had caught him, as he fled from the burning stables, had done so by means of a long chain around his neck. No one, except the master, was allowed to look after the horse, whose stable was some distance from the rest. And no one minded this; for people said that Metzengerstein himself turned pale, and stepped back, when the eyes of the horse shone with a bright and terrible light—a human light, fierce and full of meaning.

Among all the servants at the Hall, none doubted the great love which existed between their master and this nameless animal; none, that is, except a boy-servant, whose opinions were not at all important. This boy was foolish enough to say that Metzengerstein never climbed into the saddle without a slight trembling of the limbs. The boy also said that, when his master returned from every long ride, there was a look of the greatest evil in every line of his face.

One stormy night Metzengerstein woke from a heavy sleep and rushed like a madman from his room to the stables. He jumped upon the horse and raced away into the depths of the forest. This sort of behaviour was quite common. When he had been absent for several hours, the servants discovered that the Hall of Metzengerstein was on fire. Soon the great walls were cracking and falling in a fierce heat which was impossible to control. A large part of the building had already been destroyed when the flames were first seen. And now the people of the neighbourhood could do nothing but stand and watch in silent and astonished wonder.

Suddenly, up the long path which led from the forest to the main entrance of the Hall, a horse and rider flew at a speed never before seen on earth. The horseman struggled with all his strength to control the animal. His face was a picture of pain; but no sound came from his lips, which were bitten through in his terrible fear. One moment the sound of the horse's feet rang out above the roaring of the flames and the crashing of the storm; the next, both horse and rider rushed into the flaming building, and far up the staircase into the white heat of the fire.

The wind immediately grew calm. The building still burned, and now a stream of extraordinary light shot into the quiet air. A cloud of smoke settled over the Hall in the clear, immense figure of—a horse.

THE MURDERS IN THE RUE MORGUE

I HAVE ALREADY given you an example of the extraordinary qualities of mind of my friend C. Auguste Dupin.[1]

During the spring and part of the summer of 18—, he and I shared a house in Paris, in a quiet part of the Faubourg St. Germain. It was our habit, at this time, to stay indoors for most of the day, and to take long walks after dark, through the wild lights and shadows of the city. We gained a good deal of quiet enjoyment from this simple pleasure. It was at night, or in darkness (as I have said before) that Dupin found his mind most active, his power of reasoning at its best, and his ability to observe extraordinarily sharp.

We were walking one night down a long dirty street, on the east side of the city. We were both, it seemed, deep in thought; for neither of us had spoken a word for at least fifteen minutes. All at once Dupin broke the silence with these words:

"He is a very little fellow, that's true, and would do better in a lighter play."

[1] In *The Stolen Letter*.

"There is no doubt about that," I replied at once; for I had not noticed at first how strange it was that Dupin knew my thoughts. But a moment later I felt most astonished.

"Dupin," I said, seriously, "I do not understand this at all. I can hardly believe my ears. How did you know that I was thinking about . . . ?" Here I paused, to see if he could complete my question.

" . . . about the actor, Chantilly," he said, "why do you pause? You were thinking that he is too small for a serious play."

I must admit that that was exactly the subject of my thoughts. Chantilly was a shoe-maker of the Rue St. Denis, who had suddenly gone mad on acting. He had attempted the part of King Xerxes in the play of that name. He had been severely attacked by the theatre critics.

"Tell me," I cried, "how you have been able to reach into my mind like this."

"It was the fruit-seller," replied my friend, "who made you feel sure that Chantilly was not tall enough for Xerxes."

"The fruit-seller!—you astonish me—I know no fruit-seller at all."

"The man who nearly pushed you over as we entered the street—it may have been fifteen minutes ago."

I now remembered that, in fact, a tradesman who carried a large basket of apples upon his head had struck against me by accident, as we passed from the Rue C—— into the street where we were. But I could not possibly understand how this was connected with Chantilly.

"I will explain," said Dupin, "so that you will understand it all clearly. We had been talking of horses, I believe, just before leaving the Rue C——. This was our last subject of discussion. As we crossed into this street, the fruit-seller pushed you onto a pile of flat stones, which stood at a place where the road is being repaired. You stepped upon a broken piece, slipped, and twisted your foot. You turned to look at the pile, appeared to be a little annoyed, and then continued in silence.

I did not take particular notice of what you did, but I happened to observe some of your actions.

"You kept your eyes on the ground, and soon we came to a part of the road where the new stones had already been laid in a peculiar pattern. This pattern reminded me of an old Greek idea of the positions of certain stars in the heavens. And, as we discussed this subject not very long ago, I thought that you would be reminded of it also. I felt that you could not avoid looking up at the stars. You did look up; and I was now quite sure that I had followed your thoughts. But in that bitter attack upon Chantilly, which appeared in yesterday's newspaper, the writer said that he was 'a falling star which shines for a moment, and is then gone for ever.' Just then, as you were looking up, a star moved quickly across the sky. It was clear, therefore, that you would connect the star with Chantilly. I saw a little smile pass over your lips, as you thought of the poor shoe-maker's failure. Until then you had bent forward as you walked; but now I saw you straighten yourself to your full height. And I was certain that you were thinking of the shortness of Chantilly. At that moment I said that, as he was a very little fellow, he would do better in a lighter play."

Not long after this, we were reading an evening newspaper, when we saw the following:

"EXTRAORDINARY MURDERS. About three o'clock this morning, the people living in the Rue Morgue were disturbed by terrible cries which came from the fourth floor flat of Madame L'Espanaye, and her daughter, Mademoiselle[1] Camille L'Espanaye. After breaking open the street-door, which was locked, eight or ten of the neighbours entered, with two policemen. By this time the cries had stopped. As the party rushed up the stairs, two or more rough voices were heard, arguing angrily. The sounds seemed to come from the upper part of the house. As the third floor was reached, these

---

[1]Mademoiselle: Miss (French).

sounds also stopped, and everything was quiet. The party hurried from room to room. They had to force the door of a large back room, which was found locked, with the key inside. A terrible sight met their eyes when they entered this room.

"The room was in great disorder; the furniture was broken and thrown about in all directions. On one of the chairs there was an open razor, covered with blood. Two or three handfuls of thick grey human hair lay near the fire-place. This hair seemed to have been pulled out by the roots; for small pieces of flesh were sticking to it. On the floor the party found four gold coins, an ear-ring, three large silver spoons, and two bags, containing nearly four thousand francs in gold. The drawers of a desk were open and seemed to have been searched, although many things still remained in them.

"There was no sign of Madame L'Espanaye. But, as the fireplace was dirty and much disturbed, the chimney was examined. It is terrible to say that the body of the daughter, head downwards, was dragged from it. It had been forced up the narrow opening for several feet. The body was quite warm. The skin was broken in many places, probably by the violence with which it had been pushed up and pulled down. There were deep scratches on the face, and clear marks of finger-nails around the neck. It looked as if the girl had been killed by pressure around the throat.

"After a thorough search of every part of the flat, the party went downstairs, and into a small yard at the back of the building. There they found the body of the old lady, with her throat cut. In fact, it was so completely cut that the head fell off, as soon as they tried to lift her.

"So far, nothing has been found which might help to solve this terrible mystery."

The next day's papers gave this further information.

"*The Murders in the Rue Morgue*. Many people have been questioned about this crime, but the police have discovered nothing really helpful. We give below the statements that have been made.

"*Pauline Dubourg* said that she had known Madame L'Espanaye and her daughter for three years. She had done the washing for them during that time. The two ladies seemed to be very close and loving companions. She believed that Madame L. had money in the bank. Had never met anyone in the house when she called for the clothes or took them back. Was sure that they had no servant. The lower floors of the building were not used.

"*Pierre Moreau*, shopkeeper, said that he had sold small quantities of tobacco to Madame L'Espanaye for nearly four years. The two ladies had lived in the house, where the bodies were found, for more than six years. The house was the property of Madame L. The old lady was childish. Witness had seen the daughter five or six times during the six years. The two lived a very quiet life, but were said to have money. Had never seen any person enter the house, except the old lady and her daughter, a tradesman once or twice, and a doctor about eight or ten times. The house was a good house—not very old. The shutters[1] over the windows were always closed, except those of the large back room on the fourth floor.

"*Isidore Musèt*, policeman, said that he was called to the house about three o'clock in the morning, and found twenty or thirty people, trying to get in. Forced open the door with an iron bar. The cries continued until the door was opened—and then suddenly stopped. They seemed to be the cries of some person (or persons) in great pain—were loud and long, not short and quick. Witness led the way upstairs. On reaching the first floor, heard two voices in angry argument—one a low, rough voice, the other much higher—a very strange voice. The first voice was that of a Frenchman. Was certain that it was not a woman's voice. Could distinguish several French words. The second voice—the high one—was that of a foreigner. Could not be sure whether it was the voice of a man or of a

---

[1]shutter: a wooden covering for a window, used to keep out light.

woman. Could not properly hear what was said, but believed that the language was Spanish. The state of the room and of the bodies was described by this witness as we described them yesterday.

"*Henri Duval*, a neighbour, and by trade a metal-worker, said that he was one of the party who first entered the house. Agrees with the witness, Musèt, in general. Knew Madame L. and her daughter. Had spoken to both frequently. Was sure that the high voice was not that of either of the dead women. Thinks that it was the voice of an Italian. Was certain that it was not French. It might have been a woman's voice. Witness had no knowledge of the Italian language, but believed, by the sound, that the speaker was an Italian.

"—— *Odenheimer*, restaurant-keeper. This witness could not speak French. The following is a translation of what he said. Is a native of Holland. Was passing the house at the time of the cries. They lasted for several minutes—probably ten. They were long and loud—very terrible indeed. Was one of those who entered the building. Was sure that the high voice was that of a man—of a Frenchman. Could not distinguish the words spoken. They were loud and quick—unequal—and spoken, it seemed, in fear as well as in anger.

"*Jules Mignaud*, bank manager, said that Madame L'Espanaye had some property. Had opened an account at his bank in the spring of the year—(eight years before). The old lady frequently paid small amounts into her account. On the third day before her death, had taken out four thousand francs in gold. A clerk had carried the money home for her.

"*Adolphe Le Bon*, bank clerk, said that at noon three days before the murders, he went with Madame L'Espanaye to her house with the four thousand francs, contained in two bags. Mademoiselle L. opened the street-door, and took one of the bags from his hands. The old lady took the other. He then bowed and left. Witness did not see any person in the street at the time. It is a quiet street.

"*William Bird*, tailor, said that he was one of the party who entered the house. Is an Englishman. Has lived in Paris for two years. Was one of the first to go up the stairs. Heard the voices in argument. The rough voice was that of a Frenchman. The high voice was very loud—louder than the other. Is sure that it was not the voice of an Englishman. Seemed to be that of a German. Might have been a woman's voice. Witness does not understand German. Also heard the sounds of a struggle—a scraping sound.

"Four of the above-named witnesses were later questioned again. They agreed that the door of the room where the body of Mademoiselle L.. was found, was locked on the inside when the party reached it. Everything was perfectly silent. When the door was forced, no person was seen. The windows, both of the back and front room, were closed and firmly fastened on the inside. A door between the two rooms was shut but not locked. Another door leading from the front room into the passage was locked, with the key on the inside. A small room in the front of the house, on the fourth floor, at the end of the passage, was unlocked; it was full of old beds, boxes and so on. These were carefully searched. The whole house was very carefully examined. Brushes were pushed up and down the chimneys. A small door, leading to the roof, was nailed very firmly shut, and had clearly not been opened for years.

"*Alfonzo Carcio*, wood-worker, said that he lives in the Rue Morgue. Is a native of Spain. Was one of the party who entered the house. Did not go upstairs. Does not like excitement. Heard the voices in argument. The low voice was that of a Frenchman. The high voice was that of an Englishman—is sure of this. Does not understand the English language, but judges by the sound.

"*Alberto Montani*, shopkeeper, said that he was among the first to go upstairs. Heard the two voices. Distinguished several words. One of the speakers was a Frenchman. The other voice spoke quickly and not clearly. Thinks it was the voice of a Russian. Witness is an Italian. Has never spoken to a native of Russia.

"Several witnesses were examined twice. They all said that

the chimneys of all the rooms on the fourth floor were too narrow for a human being to pass through. There is no back-entrance or staircase by which anybody could have left the building while the party went up the front stairs. The body of Mademoiselle L'Espanaye was so firmly stuck in the chimney that it could not be got down until four or five of the party pulled together.

"*Paul Dumas*, doctor, said that he was called to examine the bodies about five o'clock in the morning. They were both then lying in the room where Mademoiselle L. was found. The body of the young lady was badly marked and scratched. Witness believed that these marks and scratches, except those around the neck, were caused when the body was pushed by force up the chimney. There were clear marks of fingers upon the throat. The face was pale blue in colour. The eye-balls stood out from the head. The tongue had been partly bitten. A large blue mark was discovered upon the stomach. This may have been caused by the pressure of a knee. In the opinion of Monsieur Dumas, Mademoiselle L'Espanaye had been killed by pressure upon the throat, which prevented her from breathing. The body of the mother was very badly cut. All the bones of the right leg and arm were broken. All the bones on the right side of the chest were broken. A heavy bar of iron, the leg of a table, or any large, heavy weapon, would have produced these results if it had been used, with great force, to attack the woman. The head of Madame L'Espanaye, when it was seen by the witness, was entirely separated from the body. The throat had certainly been cut with some very sharp instrument—probably with a razor.

"Nothing more of importance was discovered, although several other persons were questioned. Such a mysterious murder has never happened in Paris before—if, indeed, this is a murder. The police have no idea at all how to solve the problem."

The evening paper said that the police had arrested the bank clerk, Adolphe Le Bon, and imprisoned him; but there was nothing new to report about the crime.

Dupin seemed very interested in this affair, and later that evening he spoke to me about it.

"The Paris police," he said, "are rather stupid. They search, and examine, and question as if there is only one kind of crime—and one kind of criminal—in the world. They are active and patient, but when these qualities bring no results, their inquiries fail. Vidocq, for example, who used to be the Chief of Police, was a good guesser, and a hard-working man. But he had never trained himself to think clearly. He believed that by having many thoughts about a problem, he was certain to arrive at the correct one. He examined a thing too closely. He would then see one or two points very clearly, but he would lose sight of the matter as a whole. Vidocq often failed because he never knew the kind of inquiry to make; he never knew when to examine in a general way or in detail.

"Let us look at these murders for ourselves. You will find that it can be very interesting. Besides, I know this man Le Bon. He was once very helpful to me, and I should like to help him if I can. Let us go and see this house in the Rue Morgue; I should like to see it with my own eyes. We both know G——, who is still the Head of the police. We shall have no difficulty in getting the necessary permission."

When we had arranged the matter with the Chief of Police, it was still light enough for us to go at once to the Rue Morgue. We found the house easily; for there were many people looking up at the closed shutters from the opposite side of the street. Before going in we walked up the street, and round to the back of the house. Dupin examined the whole neighbourhood, as well as the house, with the closest attention.

At last we came again to the front of the building, where we showed our letter of permission to the officer in charge. We went upstairs—into the room where the body of Mademoiselle L'Espanaye had been found, and where both bodies still lay. Everything was as the newspaper had described it. Dupin carefully examined the room, the furniture and even the bodies. He gave particular attention to the doors and windows.

We then went into the other rooms, and into the yard, and a policeman stayed with us all through the visit. Dupin's examination lasted until it was quite dark, when we left the house. On the way home my companion called at the office of one of the daily papers.

The habits of my friend were often very strange. He said nothing further about the murder until noon the next day. He then asked me, suddenly, if I had noticed anything peculiar at the scene of the deaths.

"No, nothing peculiar," I said; "nothing more, that is, than we both read in the newspaper."

"The paper," he replied, "has merely reported what everyone knows. It seems to me that this mystery should be easy to solve because it is extremely unusual; it is so very different from any ordinary crime. The police are puzzled because they can find no reason—not for the murder itself—but for the unnecessary force that was used in the murder. They are puzzled, too, about the voices that were heard in argument. No one was found upstairs, except the murdered woman—and there was no way of escape, except by the stairs. Then there was the body, pushed up the chimney; and the old lady's head—almost completely cut off. The police think that all these extraordinary things are difficulties. But they are not. It is because of these differences from the ordinary that the murder can easily be solved. The question we must ask is not 'what has happened', but 'what has happened that has never happened before'."

"I am now waiting," Dupin went on, "for a person who knows a great deal about these deaths, although he may not be responsible for them himself. I do not think that he is guilty of any crime. Because I believe this, I have great hopes of solving the whole problem."

I looked at my friend in silent astonishment.

"I expect to see the man here," said Dupin, "—in this room, at any moment. If he comes, we shall have to keep him here. Take this gun; I have one also; and we both know how to use them, I think."

I took the weapon, hardly knowing what I was doing; and Dupin continued his explanation.

"It was the voices, of course—the voices heard in argument—that gave me my first idea. All the witnesses agreed about the rough voice; it was the voice of a Frenchman. But the high voice—the one that spoke quickly and unequally —must have been a very strange voice indeed. An Italian, an Englishman, a Dutchman, a Spaniard and a Frenchman tried to describe it; and each one said that it sounded like the voice of a foreigner. The Italian thought it was the voice of a Russian, although he had never spoken to a native of Russia. The Englishman believed it to be the voice of a German, and 'does not understand German'. The Dutchman was sure that it was a Frenchman who spoke, but this witness 'could not speak French'. The Spaniard 'is sure' that it was the voice of an Englishman, but 'judges by the sound', as he 'does not understand the English language', One Frenchman believed that the language spoken was Spanish. Another thought that the speaker was Italian. How strange that people from five countries in Europe could recognize *nothing* familiar in that voice! It was unusual, too, that only *sounds* seem to have been made by that strange speaker; no *words* were distinguished.

"Even before we went to the house," said Dupin, "I had a strong suspicion about that voice; it showed me quite clearly what I ought to look for. The next question was how the killers escaped from the building. Madame and Mademoiselle L'Espanaye were not murdered by spirits. They were murdered by beings of flesh and blood, who had somehow escaped. How? Fortunately, there is only one way of thinking about this; and it must lead us to the right answer. Let us consider, one by one, the possible ways of escape. We must look only in the large back room, where the body of the daughter was found, or in the room joined to it. If the criminals had tried to escape from the third room, or from the passage, they would have been seen by the party on the stairs. The police have broken up the floors, the ceilings, and part of the walls, and have found no secret doorways. I do not trust their eyes; so I searched with my own. There was, then, no secret way out. Both doors leading to the passage were locked, with the keys on the inside. Let us look at the chimneys. These are of ordinary width for eight or ten feet above the fire-places. But they become very narrow at the roof, and would not allow the body of a large cat to pass through. Only the windows remain. No one could have escaped through the windows of the front room without being seen by the crowd in the street. The killers must have left, then, through the windows of the back room. The police believe that this is impossible, because the windows were found closed on the inside. We know that those windows are the only possible way of escape.

"There are two windows in the room. The lower part of one of them is hidden by the bed, which is pushed closely up against it. The other one is clear of all furniture, and this window was found tightly fastened on the inside. Even the combined strength of several policemen failed to open it. A large hole had been made in its frame, and a thick nail was found fixed in this hole, nearly to the head. The other window showed the same sort of nail in the same sort of hole; and a determined attempt to open this window also failed. The police were now satisfied that the killers had not escaped through the windows. They therefore considered it unnecessary to take out the nails and open the windows.

"My own examination of these things was more careful— because I was certain that they had escaped in this way. I said to myself, 'The murderers did escape from one of these windows. But they could not have fastened them again, as they were found fastened, from the inside. Yet they were fastened. They must, then, be able to fasten themselves; there is no other explanation.' I went to the window that was clear of all furniture, and took out the nail. I tried to raise the window, but, as I had expected, it would not move. There must be, then, a hidden spring. After a careful search, I found it, and pressed it. There was now no need for me actually to open the window.

"I put the nail back into the hole, and looked at it carefully. A person going out through this window might have closed it after him, and the spring would have held it shut; but the nail could not have been put back. It was certain, therefore, that the killers had escaped through the other window. I climbed on the bed and examined the second window. The spring, as I had expected, was exactly the same as the first one. Then I looked at the nail. It was as thick as the other, and seemed to be fixed in the same way—driven in nearly up to the head.

"You will say that I was puzzled; but if you think so, you have not understood my reasoning. I could not be puzzled. There was no weakness anywhere in my argument. I had followed the secret to its end— and that end was the nail. It looked exactly the same as the first nail, as I say; but this fact was not at all important. The main thing was that the mystery ended here. 'There must be something wrong,' I said, 'with the nail.' I touched it; the head, with about a half-inch of metal, came off in my fingers. The rest of the nail was in the hole, where it had at some time been broken off. I put back the head in its place, and it looked exactly like a perfect nail; the broken part could not be seen. Pressing the spring, I gently raised the window a few inches. The head of the nail went up with it. I closed the window, and the appearance of the whole nail was again perfect.

"The mystery, so far, was now solved. The killer had escaped through the window behind the bed. He had shut the window after him, or allowed it to shut itself, and it had become fastened by the spring. The police thought that it was the nail which held the window shut, and they had looked no further.

"The next question was how the murderers had reached the ground. Now I am sure that they entered and left the room in the same way; so let us first find out how they entered. When

97

we walked around the building, I noticed a pipe which carries rainwater from the roof. It is about five and a half feet from the window. No one could have reached the window from the top of this pipe. But the shutter is as wide as the window—about three and a half feet—and made in the form of a single door. If this shutter were swung wide open, right back to the wall, it would reach to within two feet of the pipe. An active and courageous robber might have stretched across from the pipe, and taken a firm hold of the shutter. He could then let go his hold of the pipe, and he would be hanging on the inside face of the shutter. Then, pushing boldly with his feet against the wall, he might have swung the shutter so as to close it. If the window was open, he could have swung himself into the room.

"Of course a very unusual skill and courage would be required to enter the room in this way. I have shown that it is possible, but I know that it is hardly a human possibility. Now consider carefully the very unusual activity and the very peculiar voice. These two points really solve the mystery for us."

When Dupin said this, I began to understand his idea; but before I could say anything, he went on with his explanation.

"It is a waste of time to look for a reason for this crime. The police are confused by the four thousand francs in gold, which was delivered to the house three days before the murders. This money was not touched by the killers; but the bank clerk who delivered it has been arrested! It is an accident—a simple chance—that these two events happened at about the same time. Do not let the gold confuse us. Because it was not taken, we need not give it a further thought.

"Now, remembering the main points—the peculiar voice, the unusual activity and the complete absence of reason—let us consider the actual killing. Here is a woman killed by the pressure of two hands around her neck; she was then pushed up a chimney, head downwards. You must agree that this is a very strange way of hiding a body; it is quite different from our common ideas of human action. Has anyone ever before tried to hide a body in this way? Think, too, how great must have been the strength of the killer! The body had been pushed *up* the chimney so firmly that the combined efforts of several people were needed to drag it *down!*

"Turn now to the hair—to the handfuls of thick hair which had been pulled out by the roots, and which lay in the fireplace. Great force must be used to pull out even thirty or forty hairs together; but these handfuls contained, perhaps, half a million hairs. Immense power would be necessary to uproot them all at the same time. The body of the old lady shows again what terrible strength the killer used. Her throat was not merely cut, but the head was, with one blow, almost completely cut off—and the weapon was an ordinary razor.

"Of course the doctor was wrong when he said that some heavy instrument had been used upon Madame L'Espanaye. Her bones were certainly broken as a result of her fall from the window on to the stone floor of the yard. The police did not think of this, because it is connected with the nails: to them it is impossible that the windows were ever opened at all.

"I have in my hand the last, and perhaps the best, proof of my argument. I took these loose hairs from the tightly closed fingers of Madame L'Espanaye. Tell me what you think about them."

"Dupin!" I said; "this hair is most unusual—this is not human hair."

"I did not say it was," he replied. "And the finger marks on the throat of Mademoiselle L'Espanaye were also not human. Look here; I have copied them in this drawing, exactly as they appear on her throat. No human fingers could reach this distance from the thumb."

I looked at the drawing, and was forced to agree with Dupin.

"Read now," he said, "this page from Cuvier's book on the wild animals of the East Indian Islands."

It was a full description of the largest and most fierce animal belonging to the family of monkeys, a creature known as the orang-outang. The great size, strength and activity of this beast, its wild nature and its tendency to imitate, are well known. I understood at once the full mystery of the crime.

"This description of the fingers," I said, after I had read the page, "agrees exactly with your drawing. And the hair which you found seems to be the same as that of Cuvier's beast. An orang-outang must have killed the women. But how do you explain the two voices that were heard?"

"At present I cannot really explain the rough voice—which was said to be the voice of a Frenchman. But I have strong hopes of a solution. A Frenchman saw the murders; for his voice was heard upstairs. If you remember, the two voices were said to be 'in angry argument'. It is, I believe, very probable that the Frenchman was angry because the beast attacked the women. The animal may have escaped from him. He may have followed it to the house, but, for some reason, could not, or did not, catch it. It may still be free—in fact, I feel sure that it is; although I cannot explain this feeling. If the Frenchman is not really guilty of these murders, he will come to this house in answer to my advertisement. You remember that I called at the office of a certain newspaper on our way home last night; I left an advertisement there. This particular newspaper gives much news about the movement of ships, and it is always read by seamen."

Dupin handed me a paper, and I read this:

CAUGHT—In the Bois de Boulogne,[1] early in the morning of the —— (the morning of the murder), a very large, yellow-brown orang-outang of the East Indian kind. The owner (who is a sailor, belonging to a Spanish ship), may have the animal again if he can describe it correctly. A few small expenses must be paid. Call at No. ——, Rue ——, Faubourg St. Germain.

"How do you know," I said, "that the man is a sailor from a Spanish ship?"

"I do not know," replied Dupin. "I am not sure of it. Look

[1]Bois de Boulogne: the name of a park in Paris.

at this small piece of ribbon which I found at the bottom of the pipe, behind Madame L'Espanaye's house. It is a little greasy, and I think it has been used for tying up the hair in one of those long tails, which sailors are so fond of. Also, this knot is one which few people, besides sailors, can tie; and it is common only in Spain. Now, if I am wrong about this ribbon, no great harm has been done. The man will think that I have made a mistake in some detail about the animal, and it will not trouble him. But if I am right, a great advantage will be gained. The man will probably say to himself: 'I am not guilty of this murder. I am poor. My orang-outang is a valuable animal—to me it is worth a fortune. Why should I lose it through a foolish fear of danger? It was found in the Bois de Boulogne, which is far from the scene of the crime. How can anyone know that an animal killed those women? The police have failed to solve the problem. Even if they suspect an animal, there is nothing to prove that I saw the murder; there is nothing to prove me guilty. Above all, I am known. The person who advertised describes me as the owner of the beast. I am not sure how much he knows. If I do not claim this valuable animal, some suspicions may easily arise. I do not want to call attention either to myself or to the beast. I will visit the man, get the orang-outang, and keep it shut up until this matter has been forgotten.' "

At this moment we heard a step upon the stairs.

"Be ready," said Dupin, "with your gun, but do not use it or show it until I give a signal".

There was a knock at the door of our room.

"Come in," said Dupin, in a cheerful voice.

A man entered. He was a sailor, clearly— a tall, strong-looking person, with a happy, honest expression. His face, greatly sunburnt, was more than half hidden by a beard. He had with him a heavy stick, but seemed to carry no other weapon. He bowed to us, and wished us "good evening," in a voice which showed that he was a native of Paris.

"Sit down, my friend," said Dupin. "I suppose you have

called about the orang-outang. He is, indeed, a very fine beast, and no doubt a valuable one. How old do you say he is?"

The sailor drew a long breath of relief, and then replied calmly:

"I have no way of knowing—but he can't be more than four or five years old. Have you got him here?"

"Oh no; we have no place to keep him here. He is at a stable in the Rue Dubourg. You can get him in the morning. Of course, you can describe him for us—to prove that you are the owner?"

"Oh yes, sir. And I'm very willing to pay you a reward for finding the animal—that is to say, anything reasonable."

"Well," replied my friend, "that is very good of you. Let me think!—what should I have? Oh! I will tell you. My reward shall be this. You must give me all the information you can about these murders in the Rue Morgue."

Dupin said the last words very quietly. Just as quietly, too, he walked towards the door, locked it, and put the key in his pocket. He then took the gun from his coat, and laid it, without the least hurry, upon the table.

The sailor's face grew red; he got up quickly, and took hold of his stick. The next moment he fell back into his seat, trembling violently. He said nothing. I felt very sorry for him.

"My friend," said Dupin, in a kind voice, "do not be afraid. We shall not harm you. I give you my word, as a gentleman, and as a Frenchman, that we do not intend to harm you. I know quite well that you are not responsible for the deaths of the two women, but it would be foolish for you to say that you know nothing about them. The position at present is this: you have done nothing which you could have avoided— nothing to bring guilt upon yourself. You did not even rob, when you might have robbed easily enough. You have nothing to hide. At the same time, you are a man of honour, and you are bound by that honour to confess all that you know. There is a man in prison at this moment, charged with the crime of murder; he should be set free."

The sailor looked less anxious, as Dupin said these words, although his expression of happiness had completely gone.

"With God's help," he said, after a pause, "I will tell you all I know about this affair; but I do not expect you to believe even a half of what I say—I would be a fool indeed if I did. I am not guilty, and I will tell you everything, even if I die for it."

What he told us was this. He had caught the orang-outang while he was in the East Indian Islands. With great difficulty, he had brought the beast back to France, with the intention of selling it. He had locked it safely, as he thought, in a spare room of his house in Paris.

Very early in the morning of the murder, he had returned from a party, to find that the animal had broken out of its room. It was sitting in front of a looking-glass, razor in hand, trying to shave. When he saw such a dangerous weapon in the hands of such a wild beast, the man picked up a whip, which he often used to control the creature. The animal immediately rushed out of the room, down the stairs, and through an open window into the street. It was still holding the razor.

The Frenchman followed in despair. The streets were very quiet, as it was nearly three o'clock in the morning. The man had nearly caught up with the beast, when it turned into a narrow street behind the Rue Morgue. There its attention was attracted by a light shining from the open window of Madame L'Espanaye's flat. The orang-outang ran to the house, saw the pipe, and climbed up with astonishing speed. When it reached the top of the pipe, it sprang to the open shutter, and swung itself straight on to the bed. The shutter was kicked open again by the beast as it entered the room. The whole move-ment—from the ground to the bed—did not take a minute.

The sailor, meanwhile, felt both relieved and anxious. He had strong hopes now of catching the animal, as it could hardly escape from the building, except by the pipe. At the same time, he was troubled by what it might do in the house. After a moment he decided to follow the beast. Being a sailor,

The orang-outang seized madame L'Espanaye by the hair

he had no difficulty in climbing the pipe. But when he arrived as high as the window, which was far to his left, he could go no farther. All he could do was to bend over, and watch what was happening inside the room. What he saw gave him such a shock that he nearly fell from the pipe. Madame L'Espanaye and her daughter had been sorting out some clothes from a drawer when the animal sprang upon them. Now those terrible cries were heard, which woke up the neighbours in the Rue Morgue.

The orang-outang seized Madame L'Espanaye by the hair, as if to shave her face. She fought madly, and angered the creature. With one determined stroke of the razor, it nearly cut off her head. The sight of blood made the beast mad, and it fell upon the body of the girl. Grinding its teeth and flashing fire from its eyes, it pressed its terrible fingers in her throat, and kept its hold until she died. Then the orang-outang turned, and saw the face of its master outside the window. Its anger immediately changed to fear— fear of the whip. It rushed about, throwing down and breaking the furniture as it moved. It searched madly for a hiding-place for the bodies. It seized first the body of the girl, and pushed it up the chimney, where it was found. Then it picked up that of the old lady, and immediately threw it through the window.

The sailor, shocked and afraid, had tried to calm the animal. His words, with the fierce sounds of the beast, were heard by the people who entered the house. But he failed completely. Shaking with fear, he slid down the pipe, and hurried home at once. He hoped that he would see no more of his orang-outang.

There is little more to say. The beast must have escaped from Madame L'Espanaye's flat in the way that Dupin described. It must have closed the window after it had passed through. It was later caught by the seaman himself, and sold for a large amount of money to the Animal Society of Paris. The clerk, Le Bon, was immediately set free, as soon as Dupin had explained the facts to the Head of the Paris police. That official, though quite friendly to Dupin, was a little angry and ashamed at the result of the case. As we left his office, we heard him say that he hoped the police would, in future, be allowed to do their job without interference.

Dupin did not think that a reply was necessary.

QUESTIONS

1. William Wilson

1. Why did the writer call himself William Wilson?
2. Why did Wilson decide to tell this strange story?
3. Why were Wilson's parents unable to control their son?
4. For how long did Wilson attend his first school? And how old was he at this time?
5. Why did Wilson dislike his namesake?

6. How was Wilson's character different from that of his namesake?
7. What was peculiar about the size, appearance, birth-dates, etc., of the two Wilsons?
8. What was the particular weakness of the second William Wilson?
9. How did the namesake succeed in annoying Wilson?
10. What did the other school-boys think about the rivalry between the two Wilsons?

11. What happened when the two boys quarrelled for the last time at school?
12. What special event caused Wilson to leave the school?
13. To which school did Wilson go when he was fifteen?
14. When was the next meeting between Wilson and his namesake?
15. What did the namesake do and say on this occasion?

16. To which university did Wilson go?
17. Who was Glendinning? And why was he an ideal person from Wilson's point of view?
18. What was Wilson's plan for his last meeting with Glendinning?
19. What did Wilson's namesake advise the card players to do?

107

20. What did they find in Wilson's sleeve and pockets?
21. Where did Wilson go after leaving Oxford?
22. What was the intention of Wilson's namesake in interfering in the other's affairs?
23. Where was the last meeting between the two men?
24. What had Wilson decided to do if he should meet his namesake again?
25. Why was Wilson frightened and astonished when he looked closely at the man whom he had killed?

2. *The Gold-Bug*

1. Why had Mr. Legrand gone to live at Sullivan's Island?
2. What was the servant's name?
3. What were Legrand's amusements?
4. What time of year was it when the writer visited Legrand?
5. What had Legrand found that afternoon?
6. Where did Legrand find some paper on which to draw the bug?
7. What happened before the visitor had examined the drawing?
8. What could he see when he did examine it?
9. How did Legrand behave during the rest of the evening?
10. What did Jupiter blame for Legrand's illness?
11. What did Jupiter buy in Charleston?
12. What promise did Legrand make to his friend before they left the hut?
13. How did Legrand carry the gold-bug?
14. Where did Jupiter find the skull?
15. What did Legrand order Jupiter to do with the bug?
16. How far from the tree did they begin digging?
17. Why was the first hole in the wrong place?
18. What was the first thing they found in the second hole?

19. How big was the box?
20. How much did they think the treasure was worth?

21. Where had Legrand found the piece of skin?
22. Why did he believe that the skin was important?
23. How was the drawing of the skull brought out on the skin?
24. What was the special meaning of the drawing of a kid?
25. What happened after Legrand had washed and heated the skin?

26. Which letter occurs most often in English?
27. What is the most common word in English?
28. What was Bessop's Castle?
29. What was the meaning of a "good glass" in Kidd's language?
30. What had Kidd done to the men who had helped him to bury the treasure?

3. The Fall of the House of Usher

1. What was the state of the house and grounds?
2. Why did the writer visit Roderick Usher?
3. How many members of the family of Usher were still alive?
4. What did the writer think about the air which surrounded the house?
5. What particular signs of weakness were there in the building?

6. Whom did the visitor meet on the staircase?
7. What were Usher's chief interests?
8. What was the nature of Usher's illness?
9. Who was Lady Madeline?
10. What was peculiar about Madeline's illness?

11. How did the visitor try to cheer his friend?
12. What was the only way in which Usher could express his thoughts?

13. What did Usher believe about plants?
14. Why did Usher propose to keep his sister's body for two weeks?
15. Where did they place the body?

16. Why did the archway have a copper lining?
17. How did Usher behave following his sister's death?
18. What prevented the visitor from sleeping one night?
19. What did the visitor see when Usher threw open the window of his room?
20. How did the visitor try to calm his friend?

21. What did the visitor hear when he reached the part of the story where Ethelred kills the beast?
22. Who made these sounds?
23. Why had Usher been able to hear the sounds for several days?
24. Why was Usher afraid of seeing his sister?
25. How was the house destroyed?

4. The Red Death

1. What was the "Red Death"?
2. What were its signs?
3. What was Prince Prospero's plan to avoid death?
4. How many people went with him?
5. Why could no one enter or leave the castle?

6. What sort of life did the prince and his friends live in the castle?
7. What was the most splendid event of the year?
8. What had to be worn at this event?
9. How many rooms were used on this occasion?
10. What was peculiar about the colour of these rooms?

11. What colour was the window-glass in the seventh room?
12. How were the rooms lit?

13. What happened to the musicians when the clock struck the hour?
14. Whom did the dancers notice at midnight?
15. Why were there cries of fear and disgust?

16. What was the stranger wearing?
17. How did the prince propose to punish the stranger?
18. What happened when the stranger turned towards Prince Prospero?
19. In which room did the nobles attack the stranger?
20. What happened to the dancers when they tore off the stranger's clothing?

5. The Barrel of Amontillado

1. Why did Montresor want revenge on Fortunato?
2. What conditions are necessary if revenge is to be successful?
3. What was Fortunato's special weakness?
4. How was Fortunato dressed when Montresor met him?
5. Why was Fortunato surprised that Montresor had received a barrel of Amontillado?

6. How did Montresor persuade Fortunato to go with him?
7. Where did they go?
8. What special skill did Luchresi have?
9. Why did Montresor put on a mask and raise the collar of his coat?
10. Why was Montresor sure that his servants would not be at home?

11. Why was it necessary for them to carry lamps?
12. Why was the wine-store a damp place?
13. What did Montresor advise Fortunato to do to prevent cold?
14. What were in the store, besides bottles and barrels?
15. Where was the Amontillado supposed to be?

16. How did Montresor fasten Fortunato to the wall?
17. What had Montresor hidden under the bones?
18. What did Montresor build in the store?
19. Why did Montresor stop work for a time?
20. Why could no one hear Fortunato's cries?

21. How many rows of stones did Montresor put together?
22. Why did the lamps give less light than before?
23. How large was the opening in the wall?
24. What did Montresor blame for his feeling of sickness?
25. How were the conditions (mentioned in Question 2) satisfied in this case?

6. *The Whirlpool*

1. From where did the writer see the whirlpool?
2. What could be seen where the rocks entered the sea?
3. What were the names of the two islands?
4. What was the first sign of the whirlpool?
5. How long did the whirlpool take to form?

6. How wide was the whirlpool at the top?
7. What surrounded the whirlpool?
8. What happened to a ship that was pulled into the pool?
9. Why did the brothers go fishing on that dangerous part of the coast?
10. For how long could they fish between the tides?

11. Why had the fishermen never taken their sons with them?
12. What time did the fishermen leave the islands to go home?
13. What was the first sign of the storm?
14. How did the youngest brother lose his life?
15. Why could they not avoid rushing towards the whirlpool?

16. How had the fishermen mistaken the time?
17. For how long did the boat travel around the edge of the pool?

18. What was speaker holding on to in the boat?
19. What was his brother holding on to?
20. Why were these positions suddenly changed?

21. Where was the boat when the story-teller opened his eyes?
22. What other things were turning around the whirlpool?
23. What did the speaker notice about the speed with which these things travelled downwards?
24. How did he leave the boat?
25. How could his brother have escaped from the boat?

26. For how long did the boat travel around the pool after the speaker had left it?
27. What happened to the brother?
28. How far did the barrel sink before the whirlpool ended?
29. How was the speaker rescued?
30. Why did his friends not recognize him?

7. *The Pit and the Pendulum*

1. Why could the prisoner not hear what the judges were saying?
2. What was he most afraid of when he first stretched out his arms?
3. Why did he begin to walk around the room?
4. What did he use to mark his starting place?
5. What was beside him when he woke up after his first sleep?

6. What size did he think the room was?
7. Where was he going when he fell the second time?
8. What did he find in the middle of the room?
9. When the stone struck water, what did he see and hear above him?
10. What effect did the second bottle of water have on him?

11. What were the walls of his prison made of?
12. What were painted on the walls?
13. What position was he in when he woke up the second time?
14. How was he fastened to the bed?
15. Which parts of his body could be move?
16. Where did the rats come from?
17. What did he notice when he looked next at the roof?
18. How long was he lying on the bed?
19. What was happening to the pendulum during this time?
20. How did the rats save his life?

21. What happened to the blade as soon as he slid from the bed?
22. Where was the light coming from?
23. Why was he unable to see outside the prison?
24. In what way was he forced to go nearer the pit?
25. What happened as he was about to fall into the pit?

8. The Stolen Letter

1. Where did Dupin live?
2. Why did Dupin change his mind about lighting the lamp?
3. Why did the Head of the Paris police visit Dupin?
4. Why was the officer sure that the thief still had the letter?
5. Where was the lady when she received the letter?

6. Why had the Minister known that the letter was an important one?
7. How was it true that there was "full knowledge upon both sides"?
8. Why had the lady been unable to stop the Minister taking her letter?
9. How was the Minister using the power which the letter gave him?

10. Why had it been easy for the police to search the Minister's house?

11. How had the police searched the Minister himself?
12. Why did G—— think that the Minister was a fool?
13. How did the police examine the cushions in the Minister's house?
14. What was Dupin's advice to the police officer?
15. What did the officer read before he left Dupin's house?
16. When did the officer visit Dupin again?
17. What had the old man tried to get from Abernethy?
18. What did G—— sign and give to Dupin?
19. What did Dupin give to G——?
20. Why, according to Dupin, did the Paris police often fail?
21. What was Dupin's opinion of scientists?
22. Why had the Minister stayed away from his home at night?
23. Why did Dupin wear dark glasses when he called at the Minister's house?
24. Where was the letter when Dupin first saw it?
25. What was the appearance of the letter which Dupin saw?
26. Why did Dupin leave his cigarette box behind when he left the Minister's house?
27. Why did Dupin pay the man with the gun?
28. What did Dupin do when D—— rushed to the window?
29. Why did the lady have the Minister in her power?
30. Why was Dupin glad to defeat the Minister?

9. Metzengerstein
1. From what part of the world did this story come?
2. What did the people believe about the human soul?
3. What were the names of the two families?
4. What were William Berlifitzing's strongest feelings?
5. How old was Frederick when his parents died?

6. What was the distance around the Metzengerstein possessions?
7. What happened on the fourth day after Frederick's return?
8. What picture was Frederick looking at during the trouble?
9. What suddenly happened to the head of the horse in the picture?
10. What entered the room when Frederick opened the door?

11. Why were the servants struggling outside?
12. What mark was on the horse's head?
13. Where did the servants take the horse?
14. How did William Berlifitzing die?
15. What happened to the picture of the horse?

16. How did Frederick behave after the death of Berlifitzing?
17. What was the doctor's opinion about this behaviour?
18. When did Frederick ride the great red horse?
19. How had the servants caught the horse?
20. What sort of expression came to Frederick's face when he rode the beast?

21. Where did Frederick go for his last ride on the horse?
22. What happened to the Hall while he was away?
23. Why did the people not try to put out the fire?
24. Where did Frederick ride on his return?
25. What appeared above the roof of the Hall?

10. The Murders in the Rue Morgue
1. In what part of Paris were the two friends living?
2. Why did Dupin like to go out at night?
3. Why did the writer feel puzzled when Dupin mentioned the name of Chantilly?
4. What was Chantilly's ordinary work?
5. Why had Chantilly been attacked by the theatre critics?

6. What had the two friends been talking about as they were walking down the Rue C——?

7. What had reminded the writer of certain stars in the sky?

8. How did the writer change his manner of walking when he thought about Chantilly?

9. What part of the building in the Rue Morgue did Madame L'Espanaye live in?

10. How many voices were heard upstairs?

11. What was found near the fire-place in Madame L'Espanaye's flat?

12. How much money was found in the house?

13. Where did the searchers find the body of Mademoiselle L'Espanaye?

14. What did they find outside in the yard?

15. Which room in the flat sometimes had its shutters open?

16. What was the policeman Muset's opinion about the second voice which he had heard in the flat?

17. Where was Odenheimer born?

18. Who had carried home the money for Madame L'Espanaye?

19. What nation did William Bird belong to?

20. Why had Alfonzo Carcio not gone upstairs with the others?

21. What did the witnesses say about the chimneys of all the rooms?

22. What did the doctor say was the cause of Mademoiselle L'Espanaye's death?

23. Whom did the police arrest in connection with the crime?

24. Why did Dupin want to help the bank clerk?

25. Who gave Dupin and the writer permission to visit the flat in the Rue Morgue?

26. To what did Dupin give particular attention in the flat?

27. What did Dupin do on the way home?

28. When did he next speak to his friend about the murders?

29. What had given Dupin his first idea about the crime?
30. Why did he consider the second voice to have been a very strange voice?

31. Why was Dupin sure that the killer had escaped through one of the windows?
32. Why did the police not bother to examine the windows?
33. What had prevented the police from opening the windows?
34. Why was Dupin certain that the killer had escaped through the second window?
35. What happened to the nail in the second window when Dupin raised it?

36. How had the murderer climbed to the fourth floor?
37. How had he then reached the window?
38. What were Dupin's three main points about the crime?
39. What proofs did Dupin find of the extraordinary strength of the killer?
40. What had Dupin taken from Madame L'Espanaye's hand?

41. What was the strongest proof that the killer was an orang-outang?
42. Why did Dupin think that the owner of the beast was a seaman from a Spanish ship?
43. Why did Dupin say in the advertisement that he had found the orang-outang?
44. What price did Dupin ask for returning the animal to its owner?
45. Where had the sailor caught the orang-outang?

46. What did the sailor intend to do with the animal?
47. Why had the orang-outang climbed to Madame L'Espanaye's flat?
48. Why could the sailor not follow the beast?
49. Why had the animal tried to push the woman up the chimney?
50. What happened to the orang-outang in the end?